Summer Session
Sid Stark

Newsletter Signup

Want to stay in touch and get updates and offers? Get your FREE copy of the prequel novella *Foreign Exchange* and sign up for my newsletter by scanning the QR code below:

1

At first glance, she seemed like just a regular student.

Well, inasmuch as there was such a thing as a "regular" student at Indiana's intensive summer language program, where I was currently teaching. The students there tended to be a pretty heterogenous bunch. You had the flamboyant, and frequently gay, arts and drama students who were taking Russian because of their love for Dostoevsky or Chekhov. Next to them were the earnest, well-intentioned grad students who were trying to get their Russian up to professional speed before embarking on ambitious research projects in Azerbaijan or Kazakhstan or whatever corner of the former USSR their advisors had told them was hot on the job market right now. There was the crew-cut contingent, prepping for a career in intelligence or special forces or NASA by squeezing in a little Russian on the side. And then there was the occasional homemaker or retiree who was taking Russian as an unusual kind of hobby. All of them were smarter or tougher or *something* more than average, and they were all slightly—or very—weird. As I frequently reassured my students, in Slavic Studies we fly our freak flags high.

So in that group, Ruth Brown didn't stand out. At least not this first week. She was medium height, slightly plump, with dark wavy hair that skimmed her shoulders a little more closely than my own dark wavy hair skimmed mine. She was just plain enough to not qualify as pretty, and she wore comfortable below-the-knee skirts and a series of off-the-rack ruffled blouses that were modest rather than flattering, one for each day of the week, in neutral colors. When she leaned forward, sometimes a small gold cross and a slender gold ring, both on the same gold chain, would peek out from behind her collar, which was always buttoned up to her collarbones. Other than that, she wore no jewelry or anything that might catch the eye at all.

Her behavior was slightly more remarkable than her appearance, mainly from her unwillingness to stand out. She sat in the back and only spoke when called upon, and then only in short sentences, whispered at a range barely within human hearing. She didn't laugh at jokes. She didn't frown when the class troublemaker—there's always one—dropped to the floor and did twenty pushups in the middle of our review of case endings. She didn't argue with me when I said everyone had to attend all the extracurricular lectures, films, and language tables. She didn't talk on at rapturous length about her research. In fact, by Friday of our first week together, I still didn't know what her research was about, or if she was even doing any. She looked a little too old to be an undergrad, but young for a grad student. Why she was studying Russian I didn't know. The only really positive statement I could make about her was that she got perfect grades on the daily quizzes.

I mentally classed her with the other grad students, who tended once you scratched the surface to be the biggest social misfits, and assumed she wouldn't be causing me much trouble. Shyness was an irritating attribute in a student, but she seemed too self-contained to burst into tears in the middle of class, and I hoped that if I just let her do her thing, she would float silently through the entire summer session, disappearing at the end without a trace. Only she disappeared a little faster than that.

2

As soon as Ruth filed silently past me out of the classroom at noon on Friday, I stopped thinking about her. I had something much more exciting than students to think about today. Alex was coming.

The romance that had started to simmer between us last fall, when we'd been working at the same university in New Jersey, had come to a boil over the spring. He'd come down to spend spring break with me where I'd been working in Charlotte, and I'd gone up to spend a week after the end of the spring semester with him in Philadelphia. Now it was the first week of June and I was teaching in Indiana, and he was making a detour to spend the weekend with me on his way to his own summer job in Monterey, California.

He'd texted me before class to say that he was hitting the road and should be joining me in fabulous Bloomington, Indiana by mid-afternoon. I got another text just as class was letting out, telling me that he was still on track for a mid-afternoon arrival; if, that is, he didn't get lost amongst all the cornfields first.

I thought all that talk of midwestern corn was a joke, he texted. *Turns out the joke's on me. Seriously, how do people here keep from going out of their minds?*

We have to find other ways to pass the time :) I texted back.

Oh boy :) :) :) Stepping on the gas :) :) ETA now 14:30.

I sent him some smile emoticons back, gathered up my textbook, laptop, homework, and all the other bits and pieces that trail teachers wherever we go, and stepped out into the hall.

"Professor."

All the other classes were also letting out, and in the noise I didn't hear Ruth's whisper the first time. She had to repeat herself, and even grab my arm, before I noticed her.

"Can I talk to you, Professor?"

"Sure." We squeezed against the wall to let a group of grad students, so intent on their discussion of the situation in the Donbass that they didn't even see us, pass, and then stayed squeezed against the wall to avoid getting run over by a trio of extremely burly-looking guys with bald eagle tattoos who were making a run for the cafeteria before anyone else could get in line ahead of them. "What do you want to talk to me about?" I asked.

"It's..." She made an indeterminate sort of motion that was too small to be called a wriggle. "It's...can we go someplace private?"

"Of course. Let's go to my office. It's just upstairs."

"Just upstairs" was still a longish walk. Ballantine Hall, where the Russian classes and offices were located, was, like most other buildings on the Indiana campus, built to oversize proportions. Walking around the campus was like being a child in a giants' city. Going from my classroom on the fourth floor to my office on the fifth floor was a significant hike.

And once we got there, the office was full of other instructors. Ruth took one look at them, shook her head, and whispered, "Can we meet later, professor?"

"Of course. When would be good for you?"

"Like...after lunch? At two? Or three?"

"I'm afraid I'll be busy then." I made some rapid calculations of how long I should devote to Alex before running off to meet with a student. He'd probably want to tour the campus after we'd gotten our first greeting—"greeting"—out of the way, right? "What about later?" I asked. "Like five?"

She shook her head. "I've got...I guess you'll be busy over the weekend?"

"It's an intensive program. We'll all be working. I'd be happy to meet with you tomorrow morning," I said, only lying a little bit.

"Um...okay. Can we...do you think the classroom will be private?"

"It should be. Tomorrow in the classroom? Say, 10:00am?"

"Um, okay, I guess."

"Ten it is," I said, trying to sound enthusiastic without being manically chipper about meeting a student on a Saturday morning.

"Thanks, Professor." She didn't seem very thankful, but she never sounded like much of anything. She turned and left without offering any other suggestions, so I took it as a date.

3

I tried to hightail it out of there as soon as she was gone, but Masha, Sveta, and Lena, three of my friends/colleagues who shared my office, saw me by the door and invited me to join them for an evening of drinking before I could escape. The summer program was the biggest social event of the year for most of us instructors, and also required significant amounts of alcohol to make the teaching tolerable. Going out drinking on Fridays, and sometimes also Saturdays and Sundays, was a tradition.

"I'll see," I told them. "I've got a friend visiting. I don't know what he'll want to do."

"*He?*" said Sveta. "A *man*?"

"Yes," I confessed.

"Like a *boyfriend*?"

"More or less, yes."

"Oooooh, Inna! How did this happen? Tell us everything!"

"I'll tell you everything on Monday," I said. "Right now I have to go."

There was some more oohing and aahing over that. As I walked away, I heard Masha, the closest of my friends there, saying to the others, "Well, you remember how it was after Dima dumped her...but then she found this new guy, this American..."

I went out of earshot just as a spirited debate broke out over the relative merits of American versus Russian men. It was a topic that afforded a lot of scope for discussion, and we'd discussed it at length on many previous occasions. They'd probably want my insight on Monday. But now I had to get home in time to tidy the house before Alex's arrival.

Not that there was so very much tidying to do. I was naturally neat, and most of my stuff was in storage back in Charlotte, waiting to be shipped down to Georgia for the job I would be starting there in the fall. But I still felt obliged to do what I could to make my less-than-luxurious living situation as palatable as possible.

I was subletting a room in one of the old, rundown houses that filled Bloomington. The good thing about the Bloomington real estate market was that it was affordable. The bad thing was that it was mainly slums of a particular, collegiate sort. There were a lot of houses and apartments that had once been nice. After decades of being rented out to undergrads, they were filthy and falling apart. The house I was currently living in had probably been lovely eighty or ninety years ago. Now it needed to be condemned. But preferably after I moved out at the end of July.

I cut across several acres of campus, exited onto Indiana Avenue, and turned right, heading north towards 12th Street, where I was currently living. It was a long walk—Bloomington was a big town for walking—so I got my phone out and started checking my email.

There was a brief message from my mom, letting me know that she and my dad were safe and were "having a blast" working for Doctors Without Borders in Syria. How nice for them. There was a message from my brother John, telling me that he couldn't take much more of this shit with our parents rushing into war zones like lunatics.

Can't stand the taste of your own medicine? I wrote back. John was a career Marine with multiple deployments to Iraq, Afghanistan, and other similarly savory places to his credit. This made me less than sympathetic when he complained about the stress of seeing other family members put themselves in danger. He was now back at Camp

Lejeune, and not enjoying it. Of course, it was a little hard to say what John would enjoy. He'd had something of a crisis after coming back from Afghanistan last winter. I wished I could help him, and maybe I had, but John had a lot of problems, many of them unsolvable by anyone other than himself.

I scrolled through more emails. Junk, junk, junk...there was an email from Dima.

4

To say that Dima and I had a fraught history would be an understatement. An understatement of near-criminal proportions. We'd been together for eight years. For a number of those eight years we'd been engaged. And then Dima had abruptly broken it off a year and a half ago.

Admittedly, there had been extenuating circumstances. Some "serious people" who were unhappy about the spotlight he and his newspaper had decided to shine on them had expressed their feelings on the subject by kidnapping me and holding me at gunpoint. Dima had broken it off with me for, he claimed, my own good, and then he'd run off to Ukraine and thrown himself into reporting from the front lines of the war there in the Donbass. We hadn't spoken for a year after that. But now we were, tentatively, back in contact.

There had been a few painful emails over the spring, and then last month Dima had written to me asking me to forgive him. Forgive him for what, I had wanted to know. For hurting me, he had said, and making decisions that affected the both of us without consulting me. I had said I forgave him, and he had written back and said that eased his mind tremendously.

I was observing the assault on Avdiivka and almost got hit by a stray shell, he wrote. *I couldn't stand the thought of dying without making things right between us, Innochka. I promised myself that if I got out alive, the first thing I'd do would be to beg your forgiveness for being such a shitty fiancé. So here I am, begging for it.*

What do you mean by "making things right between us"? I had asked.

I don't mean getting back together, if that's what you're asking. The same old problems are still there. You need to leave me behind and find someone else, someone better. But I couldn't stand the thought of dying with you hating me.

I don't hate you.

You should.

Yeah, maybe, but I don't. I forgive you. And I'm sorry.

What for?

I hurt you too.

Not on purpose.

Even so.

I don't forgive you, Inna, because there's nothing to forgive. But I want you to stay in America, far away from me and all this shit. Do you have another man yet?

Maybe?

I'm glad, Dima had written, and I hadn't heard from him for a couple of weeks. Now he had taken to checking in every few days, assuring me that he was okay and not-so-subtly fishing for information about this new man in my life.

My article about the battle at Marinka just came out, he wrote to me this time. *I'm out of there now, though, so don't worry) What are you doing this weekend? Any good plans?))*

I walked a couple of blocks while I thought about how to respond to that. Then I wrote back that I was expecting a guest.

A guest? Dima wrote back before I had gotten to the next block. *Male?*

Yes. I thought about leaving it at that, but then, curious to see how he would respond, added, *My new boyfriend.*

That's nice, Dima answered. That two-word email was followed a couple of minutes later by a slightly longer message.

I'm glad you can tell me these things, he wrote. *I wish you all the best, Inna.*

Thanks, I wrote back. *And I hope you can tell me about your life too.*

Nothing to tell))) Goodnight, Inna.

As usual, Dima had to have the last word.

5

"**F**evronia! I'm home!"

I stepped into the house that was my temporary home. No tan furry face peered out from behind the couch. Not surprising. Fevronia tended to be aloof and standoff-ish, even for a cat.

I dropped off my bags and folders on the weird glass stand that was serving as my table. The house was supposed to be furnished. Its furnishings consisted of a strange glass thing that was probably meant to hold CDs or something, an extremely worn couch of indeterminate color that had worrisome-looking stains and a broken leg, and a baby grand piano. There were no beds, chairs, or tables anywhere in the house. I had picked up an inflatable mattress my first evening in town, and was now using it as my main work area as well as my sleeping surface.

I arranged my suitcases and belongings as neatly as possible against the wall of the bedroom. I remade the bed so that it looked a little more presentable. I needed to do laundry, but there wasn't time before Alex arrived, so he'd just have to put up with me doing it while he was there. And that way he could come down into the scary laundry room at the far end of the scary basement with me. I didn't think of myself as being easily creeped out, but the basement was painted a hellish shade of IU red, interspersed with occult symbols and water stains from where it flooded every time it rained. The laundry room was a tiny alcove at the far end, and could only be reached on dry days. No doubt the whole thing was full of mold. There was no door to the basement, so I worried about Fevronia getting down into it, or strange things creeping up out of it in the middle of the night. So far neither of those things had happened, but it kept me up at night in between trains. Because, oh yes, the house was next to a train track.

Sweeping and dusting failed utterly to transform the house into a gracious home one would want to welcome guests into. Cleaning the bathroom did make the fixtures slightly less grimy, but revealed their inherent cheapness and worn state even more clearly. I hoped Alex wouldn't look too closely at anything. Of course, his own place in Philly had been pretty run-down too.

The sad fact was that between us we had two PhDs, two critical need languages, and a combined salary that would barely cover rent. So even though we were both in the second half of our thirties and in theory gainfully employed in a prestigious profession, we both lived in poverty. Although maybe that would change. We both had new jobs waiting for us in the fall. New jobs at opposite ends of the continent. Well, beggars quite literally can't be choosers.

Fevronia came slinking out from wherever she'd been hiding around the time I finished my cleaning efforts. I suspected she had taken to stalking prey in the unused bedrooms. The house was set up for four people, but I was currently the only one subletting a room in it, so I had its cavernous creepiness all to myself. At least Fevronia was keeping the mice away.

Alex's battered old car pulled up behind my battered old car at 2:45.

"Nice place," he said, getting out and surveying the yard and the sagging porch. "Very squatter's chic."

"You should see the inside." I squinted at him as he jumped up onto the porch. "You've shaved!" And indeed, the golden-brown stubble that matched his golden-brown hair was gone. His body was still fit and wiry, and his hazel eyes still had an underlying expression of intelligence and intensity, even though right now they were smiling for all they were worth.

"Vanity demanded it," he said, rubbing his chin with his hand. "I looked in the mirror yesterday and saw I was developing a gray patch. You like?"

"Very much."

"Good." He kissed me, and then pressed his newly smooth cheek against mine. "So what about the inside?" he asked when he pulled away.

He laughed at the front room with its alarming couch and baby grand piano, but only for a moment. Then he was too busy putting his arms around me to laugh at my living situation.

"Please tell me you at least have a habitable bedroom," he said into my ear.

"Almost as habitable as yours in Philly," I told him.

"That nice, huh? Well, we made that work, didn't we?"

"We sure did. Do you want to see it?"

His arms tightened around me. "Lead the way," he said.

6

Afterwards, when Alex had laughed his fill at my bedroom and particularly at the basement when he helped me haul a load of laundry down into it—"I'll be happy to take the laundry down every day, if it means christening the sheets like that," he said—I suggested we go out to eat.

"The kitchen is barely fit to cook in," I said. "And the restaurant scene here is good. What do you fancy? Korean? Japanese? Thai? Burmese? Tibetan? Turkish? Or something a little less exotic?"

"You choose."

We ended up walking down to 4th Street to survey the options there. Alex alternated between admiring the party-town vibe of everything, and filling me in on his move from Philadelphia to Monterey.

"It's such a fucking pain in the ass," he said. "At least I don't have much stuff. I just threw everything I could in my car, and tossed the rest. And I'm not planning on getting much more, at least not right away. Who knows how long I'll be there, right?"

"Right." Alex had a two-month summer job at the intensive language program in Monterey, followed by a one-year position at the DLI, the Defense Language Institute, which was in the same town. After that, where he would be was anyone's guess. The job market was fickle, and the unspoken issue that hung in the air between us was that where he would be living next year might be up to me as much as him.

"So how's it going here?" he asked. "How are the students?"

"You know, the usual. Which reminds me: I'm supposed to be meeting with one tomorrow." I filled him in on the Ruth situation, inasmuch as there was anything to fill him in on.

"She's probably got some kind of learning disability, and wants to tell you about it in private," Alex said. "You said she's super shy: maybe she's been given a waiver from speaking in class or taking oral exams."

"That does seem like the most likely explanation. Although how she's planning to do anything with her Russian, or any other language, if she can't actually speak, is beyond me."

"Yeah. But you know how it is. Education is inherently unfair, and when they try to level the playing field, half the time they end up making it worse. Now you're going to have to spend eight underpaid weeks teaching someone who shouldn't be in your class to begin with, and isn't actually going to learn anything from it."

"Yeah." We strolled on for a block in silent contemplation of the unfairness of life, and how Ruth, who probably had more than enough problems of her own, was going to cause other people, e.g., me, problems as well. Then we decided to check out the Tibetan restaurant.

7

It was a lovely early June evening, warm but not scorching the way it would be by July, so we sat out on the patio of the Tibetan restaurant and watched the people go by on 4th Street as we sampled Tibetan delicacies. It was surprisingly busy for the summer, and many of the passers-by were from my program.

"This is nice," said Alex, after I'd waved at the third group of people walking by. "It's almost like there's a social scene here for people like you and me."

"Maybe it will be the same in Monterey," I said encouragingly.

Alex shrugged. "Maybe. I'm not holding my breath. But I've been thinking..."

"Yes?"

"Now you *have* to come visit me, right? So I can show you around, just like you're showing me around Bloomington."

"I might be able to. I get out of here the last week of July, and then I have three weeks until I have to report for orientation at Crimson."

"Perfect. Just enough time for a road trip to California. Or catch a flight if you can."

"I'll have to see what they cost. Although...a road trip *does* sound like it could be fun...aw crap!"

"What is it?"

"It's some of my students! Coming in here! In fact, it's Ruth!"

I said the last in a half-whisper, and then smiled and waved at Ruth as she caught site of me. She was accompanied by Naomi, who sat next to her in class, dressed almost as modestly, and was almost as shy. Although in Naomi's case it was a bit more understandable, since she had the honor of being the lone black student in the class. Whenever someone is the lone representative of their group, whatever that group happens to be, within a larger group, there are two ways they can go: standing out for all they're worth, or fading into the background. Naomi had been trying all week for the latter, just like Ruth. I was not surprised to see them together, but I was glad, since that suggested at least they had each other for company.

I was more surprised to see them accompanied by two men on what was clearly a double date. I didn't recognize either of the men, although they both had that very fit, crew-cut look of the military contingent. Neither Ruth nor Naomi had struck me as the type to pick up a casual date for their first Friday in town, nor to allow themselves to be picked up. There must have been more to them than met the eye.

The foursome disappeared into the restaurant and then reappeared a couple of minutes later, led by a server who sat them at the table next to ours. I repressed a groan and smiled at them with my best friendly-yet-professional smile. One of the downsides about the Bloomington summer social scene was constantly bumping into your students. And while many of the students were fun, interesting people who went on to become my friends later, it was awkward to be on a date while sitting next to a student who was also on a date.

Ruth, Naomi, and I made some very stilted conversation while the two men with them waited impatiently for me to stop taking away the girls' attention. I confirmed with Ruth that we would be meeting the next morning, and then, with an internal sigh of relief, turned back to Alex.

Only Alex and I couldn't have much of a conversation. Not only did the close proximity of students put a damper on the discussion of anything intimate, but the two men with Ruth and Naomi began talking loudly as soon as I stopped, and continued talking loudly throughout the ordering, serving, and eating process. Alex and I got to hear the details of their decision to come to Indiana to study Arabic, their trip over here, their living situation—they were sharing a sublet of an apartment on 3rd Street—their first week of class, their future prospects and how much brighter they would be if they could earn a rating of 3 on the ILR (Interagency Language Roundtable) scale for Arabic, and pretty much everything else they could think of to talk about.

By the time they were well into their main course, and Alex and I were waiting for the server to bring back the check, the talk had somehow veered around to women in the military. I stifled another groan. I could already tell that this was going to be painful. Alex was looking longingly towards the restaurant entrance, as if hoping that the server would reappear, receipt in hand, and rescue us. But the restaurant was now packed full both inside and out, and our server was being run off her feet.

"Nah, they shouldn't be letting women in Special Forces units," the man across from Naomi was saying. I snuck a peek over at her, hoping to see her incinerate him in some way. But all I saw was the self-satisfied smirk on his face.

"They're bringing down standards, letting women in," said the man across from Ruth. "Women just can't keep up. Certainly not for Ranger training."

Out of the corner of my eye, I saw Ruth and Naomi both nod in silent and submissive agreement.

"The most important thing is operational ability, not politics," said the first man. "That has to be a priority, not political correctness. We need the best of the best."

"That's funny," said Alex. "Because they let men into intelligence and the medical corps."

Both men stopped and stared at him. "That's different," said the man with Naomi.

"No, it's not," said Alex. "On average, female doctors have a lower patient mortality rate than males, something you might want to remember if you ever need to get patched up after accidentally discharging your weapon. On average, females learn to speak and read at an earlier age than males. Adult females are more likely to go into language and the humanities than males, and are more likely to excel at it. And yet the Navy still had me, a male, learn Arabic, and sent me to Iraq to use it, and I'm sure my classes at the DLI will be full of males. So don't give me that shit about needing only the best of the best and women not being able to keep up. If Uncle Sam is willing to waste his training dollars on teaching you Arabic, I'm sure he can spend a little money on sending some women to Ranger school or whatever you Army people call it."

The two men opened their mouths but without having any words ready to come out of them. Just then, the server brought back Alex's credit card and the receipt.

"Thanks," he said to her, signing the receipt with a flourish. "*Tasharrafnā*," he added to the two men.

Identical looks of panicked confusion crossed their faces. I was guessing this was a vocab word they had been supposed to learn but now, in this high-stress moment, couldn't remember.

"The correct response is '*farṣa-saëda*,'" Alex told them conversationally. "No doubt if you asked any of the girls in your class, they'd be able to tell you. Maybe you could use some of that fast-twitch muscle you're so proud of to carry their bags in exchange. Are you ready to go, Rowena?"

"Yes," I said. "*Do zavtra*," I said to Ruth and Naomi, and left.

8

"I'm sorry," Alex said, once were back out on 4th Street. "I shouldn't have done that."

"No, you definitely should have," I told him. "That was everything I've always wanted to say to jerks like that, but it had a lot more impact coming from you."

"Yeah." He gave me a self-conscious smile. "I guess I'm kind of a hothead, huh? I just...I had it up to here"—he made a gesture at his neck—"with assholes who thought they were better than God because they could do one-armed pushups. I just couldn't stop myself from reminding them that there are some things that other people, including—no, *especially*—women, are better at than they are. I mean, I'm sure if they paid attention in class, they'd notice how they were getting their asses kicked by all the girls, but since they're not going to pay attention, it's going to go right over their heads. So I had to remind them. It was certainly a shock to me when I realized a girl was better than me at something, and that was just how it was going to be."

"And then what?" I asked. "What did you do about it, once you'd had that realization?"

"I worked my ass off until I was *almost* as good as her, and then I convinced her to go out with me."

I looked over at Alex in the twilight. It should have been a happy story, one that made him smile, but he was frowning and looking at the Thai restaurant we were walking past without seeing it.

"Was she the one?" I asked.

"The one what?" He still wasn't looking at me.

"The one you've mentioned, the long-distance relationship that didn't work."

"Oh. Yeah, she was the one."

"I'm sorry."

He shrugged. "Don't be." He turned, and, with a visible effort, smiled at me. "I'm here with you now, right? That's what counts. At least for me. I hope it counts for you too. Otherwise, we could go back and see if those two are still there and are looking for a real woman instead of those two dishrags they were with."

"Ruth and Naomi aren't dishrags. They're just...quiet."

"They didn't even look mad when those two guys were mouthing off like assholes. They smiled and agreed to everything they said."

"Maybe they were too scared to disagree."

"Maybe," said Alex. "But then they should have just gotten up and walked away. Or not agreed to go out with them in the first place."

"Yeah, but..." I kind of agreed with Alex. Ruth and Naomi definitely shouldn't have agreed to go out with those guys in the first place, if they didn't actually like them, or, worse, found them frightening. But they had, and I could see how they might not want to make any waves by arguing with them, or how they might be too stunned by the waves of jerkiness washing over them to be able to fight back. But to be honest, I hadn't gotten that feeling from them. I'd gotten the feeling that, inasmuch as they were expressing any emotions at all, they were glad to be with two such macho alpha males, and were happy to agree to anything they said in order to have the burden of standing up for themselves taken off their shoulders.

"I don't get it," I said out loud.

"Don't get what?"

"The attraction of men like that. Not the muscles and the uniforms and the danger; I get *that*. But I *hate* being talked down to and told what to do."

"I know you do, Rowena. It's one of the most attractive things about you."

"That sounds like damnation through faint praise. But I've never understood how women can tolerate men who boss them around and, even worse, so obviously look down on them. I mean, would *you* put up with someone who clearly thought you were their inferior?"

"I'm afraid," said Alex, "that my answer to that might be a little different than yours. I think you might have a little more self-respect than I do, Rowena."

"Really?"

"Unfortunately, yeah."

"Oh. Well, you *should* have self-respect. And so should Naomi and Ruth. And jeez! It just occurred to me. What if Ruth wants to talk to me in private tomorrow because she's being stalked, or coerced, or something, by that guy?"

"It's possible," said Alex.

"What if that's why she wanted to meet with me this afternoon: because she was being pressured into going out with him this evening, and she was afraid? And I said I couldn't meet with her until tomorrow, and then I just walked off and left her in the restaurant with him! After we made them mad!"

"After I made them mad, you mean," said Alex. "But it's more likely that it's something school-related. And for what it's worth, I got an asshole vibe off those guys, but not a rape-y vibe. Ruth and Naomi are probably safe enough, at least physically."

"I guess."

"You've already done what you can do, Rowena. You've already agreed to meet with her, and on a Saturday morning. She's a big girl: if she's got a serious problem, she needs to figure out how to solve it herself. If she really is being stalked or whatever, she needs to go to police, not her Russian instructor."

"The police are normally worse than useless in situations like that."

"Okay, fair point. But if—*if*—she's in that kind of trouble, it's still not your problem. Those guys aren't even in your program, let alone your class, right?"

"Right."

"So if—*if*—they're causing her problems beyond the mere fact of being inveterate assholes, there's not a lot you can do about it. She needs to go to the program director, who needs to have a word with them. So *if* that's what's going on, that's what you're going to tell her to do, right?"

"I just said I hated being told what to do."

Alex grinned. "And now I know you're not actually that worried."

"Yeah. I guess you did a good job of getting my mind off my problems."

We were now up around 10th Street, where there were no restaurants, only houses, most of them empty. Alex took advantage of the comparative darkness to lean over and kiss my ear. "And I hope I can do an even better job of it once we get back to that shithole you're calling a house."

"It's a deal," I said.

9

A lex managed to take my mind off things pretty well that night, and he was still feeling amorous the next morning.

"I wish I could," I told him. "But I have that meeting with Ruth at ten, and I really need to get some grading done before then."

"I'd take your declared intent to work more seriously if you weren't sitting in my lap in bed," said Alex.

"This is the only work area I have here. So either you can be my chair, or I can leave you and go work in my office."

"Chair it is, then," said Alex.

As a chair he left a lot to be desired, although having his arms around me helped dull the sting of grading my students' first chapter tests.

"I can't believe that Ruth wants to talk to me about academic problems," I said when I was done. "She got the second-highest grade on the test, after Naomi, and she's currently leading the class in written work overall. She's not going to fail, or anything even close. If she could only open her mouth in class, she'd be brilliant."

"Yeah. *If.* What time is it? Nine? Time for a little fun and good times before your meeting?"

"If by fun and good times, you mean a quick tour of campus, then yes."

"Actually, I meant something best done right here, in the bedroom."

"In that case, I'm holding out for when we get back this afternoon. I want longer than the twenty minutes I could give you right now."

"Oh boy," said Alex. "Let's get going, then. And I'll be thinking of ways to pass the time sloooowly this afternoon."

"I'll hold you to it," I said. "When I'm not holding it against you, that is."

"Is that a promise?"

"It sure is. But now we have to go."

I felt practically naked, setting off for campus with only my purse, instead of the twenty or thirty pounds of books, papers, and other sundry materials I normally carried with me.

"Nope," Alex said when I mentioned it to him. "You're fully dressed. Unfortunately. Whoa! Is that a chipmunk?"

"Probably. The whole town is completely overrun with chipmunks, rabbits, and the biggest squirrels you've ever seen."

And in fact we saw two more chipmunks, an adolescent rabbit, and a couple of monster squirrels as we walked down Indiana Avenue. Once we got onto campus we had to stop counting the wildlife, it was so abundant.

"It's kind of like being in *Cinderella,*" said Alex as we crossed one of the bridges over the Jordan River. "Although up close those squirrels are pretty scary. Are you sure they're not mutants? Are there any nuclear dumping grounds around here that might be breeding ninja turtles and shit like that?"

"I think Indiana is one of the most polluted states in the nation, especially up around Gary. But I think the squirrels achieve their size all on their own. Although maybe they've been hit by some bad magic. Some of us think that Ballantine Hall is really Hogwarts."

"Because it's a magical place of learning?"

"No, because the floor numbering system is insane. You'll find out when we get there."

We skirted around the massive Memorial Union and approached the almost equally massive structure of Ballantine Hall.

"Or maybe the squirrels have just expanded in size to fit in with their surroundings," said Alex.

"Very possible. Ready for some climbing?"

"Rock climbing?" he asked hopefully.

"Stair climbing."

"Only if you get to go first so I can ogle your ass."

"Sure...oh, hi, Naomi!" I hoped with a false hope that Naomi hadn't heard Alex's words. By the expression on her face, she had at least guessed their general context. I wondered whether having students know about my personal life would make me more or less effective as an instructor.

"Hi, Professor Halley," she said. "Are you on your way to meet with Ruth?"

"Yep. Is she around?"

"I just walked with her to the classroom. We're supposed to meet afterwards at The Pourhouse Cafe to do some studying together."

"Sounds nice."

"Yeah. And...um...I just wanted to say"—she looked over at Alex—"thanks for what you said last night. To Matt and Drew. Someone needed to." She covered her mouth. "You didn't hear me say that!"

"Yeah, I did," said Alex. "And they needed to hear that. Hope they weren't too jerky to you about it afterwards."

Naomi uncovered her mouth. Her lips lifted into the world's tiniest foxy grin. "Not once we'd smoothed things over a little, told them we appreciated them using their 'fast-twitch muscles' to carry our heavy bags and protect us from the street people of Bloomington. You just have to know how to say the right things, you know? Although my mother says I'm much too pushy with men, and I'll never get a husband...but anyway. Honestly, they're not as bad as they seem at first. They just, I don't know, have a lot of high spirits, and they were happy to be with us. They're actually pretty nice, once you get to know them. And they wanted to know more about you." She paused, waiting hopefully for Alex to fill her in on his background.

"Tell them I'm sure my faculty webpage will be up soon in the DLI's Arabic program website," Alex said. "They can look at it to their heart's content."

"So you really do speak Arabic? You're, like, a real Arabic instructor?"

"So they tell me," said Alex. He checked the time on his phone. "And now I think Professor Halley needs to get going in order to meet with Ruth."

"Oh. Yeah. *Do skorovo,* Professor Halley! Hope you can help Ruth." Naomi gave me an actual full-on smile, and walked off in the direction of Kirkwood Avenue and The Pourhouse Cafe.

10

"I see what you mean about Hogwarts." Alex was climbing up the stairs in Ballantine. Behind me, just as he'd promised, although with no apparent strain in his voice, even though we were ascending briskly up the oversized floors. Alex claimed to hate running and most forms of PT, but he loved rock climbing, so he kept himself fit for that. "What floor are we on?" he asked.

"We're on the third floor. Which is really the fourth floor. Depending on which numbering system you're using. One more floor to go. Unless you want me to whip out my faculty elevator pass and use that." Students were discouraged from using the elevators and had to request special disability accommodations to be allowed on them, but faculty got passes that enabled us to activate them. I wasn't sure how I felt about that. Of course people should take the stairs rather than the elevators if they could. But that kind of segregation and special privileging made me uneasy.

"I can make it. You spent six years here, huh? I can see why you're so fit."

"Among other reasons. Okay, here we are."

We left the oversized stairs and started down the oversized hallway. My classroom was at the opposite end of the building from where we'd entered, so it was a long walk. We passed a couple of occupied classrooms on our way, where interest meetings for the drama club and the choir were being held. On top of our other duties, instructors were expected to organize extracurricular activities.

"Oh fuck, I'm probably going to have to do something like this too," said Alex, when I explained to him what was going on in the occupied classrooms. "What the fuck am I going to do?"

"I'm running a 'dirty poetry' circle," I told him. "That's easy enough, since we hold our meetings during the regular language table hours. But some super gung-ho instructors like to stage entire plays."

"God no," said Alex. "Can I steal your idea? I just need to come up with enough dirty poetry. Does *The Rubaiyat of Omar Khayyam* count? Maybe we can compare translations. What are you doing? And is there enough material to fill an entire summer?"

"In Russian? Are you kidding? More than enough."

Alex grinned. "Care to teach me any?"

"Soon as we're done here, I can start teaching you about how Pushkin wanted to entrust to the beauteous Rebecca 'what separates Christians from the faithful Jew.'"

Alex took a beat to think about that, and then burst out laughing. He was still laughing when we entered my classroom. Which was empty.

"I guess Ruth stepped out. What time is it?"

Alex pulled out his phone. "9:55. She'll probably be here in a second. So this is it, huh? How many hours do you spend in here a week?"

"Fifteen. I teach from eight to nine and from ten to twelve Monday through Thursday, and from nine to twelve on Fridays. The students have twenty-three hours a week of class: fifteen of grammar, which is what I'm teaching; two of listening, two of phonetics, and four of conversation."

Alex made a face. "I'd sympathize, only I think I'm going to be spending even more time with my guys. I hate them already, and I haven't even met them yet."

"Surely they'll be okay. Most of mine are."

"That's because they're yours, Rowena. Mine will be fuck-ups, because I can't love and nurture them like you can."

"Sure you can. I remember what you did for Justin back at TLASC."

"Justin was special. Justin was actually a good student in a bad situation."

"So are a lot of the others."

"Maybe. Sort of. If by that you mean 'spoiled brat.'" Alex checked his phone again. "Speaking of spoiled brats, where is this Ruth?"

"I don't think she's a brat. She just maybe has some problems."

"She's late for a Saturday morning meeting with her professor."

"Maybe she's got something going on."

"Or maybe she decided to blow you off," said Alex. "Wouldn't be the first time a student's done something like this."

"Okay, fair point. Let's give her a few more minutes."

We waited till 10:15. Then I sent Alex up to check the office upstairs and see if Ruth was waiting for me there. He came back shaking his head. Just to be on the safe side, we waited until 10:30. Then, because at that point I was pretty pissed, we set off for The Pourhouse Cafe, in case Ruth had lost her nerve—"Or hooked up with some dude," said Alex cynically—and gone straight to her meeting with Naomi.

11

The cafe was only a couple of blocks from campus, but campus was big. By the time we got there, it was almost eleven. Naomi was sitting right by the front entrance, checking her phone and looking up anxiously every time someone came in the door. When she spotted us, relief and worry fought for supremacy on her face. Worry won.

"Was she really nervous, Professor?" she said quietly when I came over to her table. "I thought she'd be here by now. But she hasn't come and she hasn't texted me. Did she go straight home?"

"She didn't show up at all," I said. "And she didn't email me either."

Naomi's forehead wrinkled up in an even more worried frown. "That's weird. I walked her to the classroom myself. She was there when I left her, I'm sure of it. I offered to sit with her and wait until you showed up, but she said no, she'd rather be by herself, and she sent me on here."

"Well, she wasn't there when I got there ten minutes later. And we didn't see her anywhere in the hall or the stairs. She must have gone out the other staircase and left that way. Where do you live? If she'd gone out that way, she would have been heading towards 3rd Street."

Naomi shook her head. "We're in the A building of Willkie Quad. We always use the stairs on the other end of the building, the ones that let you out across from the chapel."

"Could she have been going to see, um"—I scrambled for the names—"Matt and Drew? Don't they live on 3rd Street?"

"Yeah, but, I mean, I don't think Ruth would do *that*. Matt seemed to think they were going out, but I mean, come on. They only met on Monday. They've only been out for dinner twice."

"More than enough time to get a spark going," said Alex.

Naomi looked affronted. "I mean, I've only known Ruth for a week too, but we clicked. We've done a lot of talking. Especially about Matt and Drew. She specifically said more than once that she wasn't the kind of girl to, you know"—now Naomi was looking charmingly embarrassed over something that many people her age would have laughed off as a joke—"with a guy after just a couple of dates. Like"—she looked even more embarrassed—"me. We're both from, um, religious families. We're Pentecostals. That's one of the reasons we clicked. We didn't want to, you know"—she lowered her voice even more—"chase men."

"Poor Matt and Drew," said Alex, not sounding very sincere.

"They said they liked that about us," said Naomi. "That we weren't, you know"—her skin was too dark to show a blush easily, but I could feel my own cheeks flushing in sympathy at the sight of her discomfort—"promiscuous," she finished in a whisper. "They said they were, you know, old-fashioned," she added more confidently. "They're Pentecostals, just like us. So that's why—well, one of the reasons—why they wanted to, you know, spend time with us. They wanted to watch out for us. This isn't a very friendly place for people like us. It's easy to stray, and the other students aren't always very understanding. Ruth...well, I guess she won't mind me telling you this, but...she wore, you know, a purity ring, but she felt so embarrassed by the way some of the students reacted to it that she took it off her first day here. She really feels out of place here, and she was so relieved that I was in her class, and then that we found Matt and Drew. Before that she was talking about quitting the program and going home early. But then Drew said he found a church here in town we could all go to, one that his pastor had recommended, so she said she'd stick around at least until we went to a service."

"Okay," I said. Now I could see the attraction between Ruth and Naomi and Matt and Drew. Whatever else they didn't have in common, they must have all felt very out of place at a party school like Indiana. "Can you give Ruth a call?" I asked. "I just want to make sure she's okay. I don't want her to feel like she couldn't come talk to me."

"Yeah," said Naomi. "She picked you because, well, you seemed a little nicer than the others. She wanted to ask you about going on a mission trip to Russia, and she thought you might not laugh at her, the way the other instructors might. But she was still really nervous. She's so shy, you know. She probably just lost her nerve and had to go hide in the ladies' room or something."

"If she's nearby, tell her to come on over and I'll talk to her right now," I said.

"Really? That's really nice of you, Professor Halley."

But Naomi let her phone ring ten times, and Ruth never picked up.

12

"Maybe her phone's dead," said Naomi. "Maybe something happened to it, and she had to go deal with that, and that's why she couldn't email you or text me or anything. Maybe she dropped it in the bathroom and it got wet and she had to run home to dry it with a hair dryer."

"That seems as likely a scenario as any," I said. "Tell you what: I've got to go to the Union to make some printouts. If you want, I can text you and then you'll have my number and you can text me, or you can give my number to Ruth and she can text me, if she shows back up in the next hour or so and still wants to meet. And just in general, ask her to let me know."

"Will do, Professor. And thanks again."

"No problem," I told her. "Have a nice Saturday, and *do ponedel'nika.*"

"Is there coffee at the Union?" Alex asked, as soon as we were out on Kirkwood Avenue and heading back to campus. "Because I gotta be honest: letting me inhale all that coffee smell without actually getting any was pretty cruel. I'm jonesing for a fix so bad I think my hands are shaking."

"There should be. You can go get some while I make some printouts. I hope I have enough printer credits."

"Let me guess: the university keeps you on a very tight budget for printouts and copies, while insisting that you do all of your testing as sit-down pencil-and-paper exams."

"It's like you know how schools work," I said. "We used to be able to use the department copier, but no more. Now we get printer credits and have to go to the print stations like we're students. We all got a set number of credits, but I have fifteen students in my group, which is twice the size of a lot of the other groups, so the standard print quota is grossly inadequate. The program director has been trying to get me more credits, but as of yesterday afternoon it hadn't worked. I'm going to give it another shot today."

"And if it's still not working?"

"I guess we'll have to experiment with alternative formats for Monday morning's vocab quiz."

"Ah yes. The whole innovation-in-teaching-because-the-technology-I'm-required-to-use-isn't-working thing."

"Yeah, exactly—oh, um, hi."

Matt and Drew were coming out of the Union, heading straight towards us. I wondered which one was Matt and which one was Drew. They looked, if not identical, then similar enough to be fraternal twins. They were both white, with light brown buzz-cut hair and hazel eyes, and they were tall and rangy and moved with the solid confidence of the extremely fit. They were both wearing khakis and t-shirts that somehow managed to look like uniforms, even though they weren't. The one on the right, who was about an inch shorter and had been with Ruth the night before, had a small silver cross in the hollow of his throat. The one on the left, who had been with Naomi, was well over six feet and had a cross tattooed in the same place.

"Look, uh, sir," said the one on the left as he drew level with Alex. "We wanted to apologize."

Alex gave him a blank look. "For what?"

"For being...you know."

"Assholes?" suggested Alex.

They both grinned. "Yeah, that. We shouldn't have...we were just blowing off steam, running off our mouths. You were right to call us out on it."

"It's just tough," said the one on the right. "Always having to pick up the girls' slack in PT."

"Yeah," said Alex. "But that's what I was saying: they're always having to pick up your slack in class. Only you don't even see it."

"Yeah. I, um, I guess that's right," said the one on the left. "Anyway, we just wanted to say thanks. For, you know, taking the time to give us your perspective. And, uh..."

"We were wondering if we could, like, buy you a coffee or something," said the one on the right. "'Cause we'd, like, we'd really like to hear about Iraq."

"We might be, like, deploying somewhere after this," said the one on the left. "And we'd, like, you know, appreciate some, uh, insight, I guess."

"I don't know how much insight I can give you," said Alex. "But if you're buying coffee, I'll give you anything I can."

Both men smiled in relief. "I'm Drew," said the one on the left. "Matt," said the one on the right.

"Doctor Miller," said Alex. There was a round of handshakes, and then the three of them headed off to the Union Starbucks, leaving me to contemplate the hierarchical nature of male behavior. Matt and Drew had been more than happy to lord it over Ruth and Naomi, and had attempted to stand up to Alex, but as soon as he had so much as hinted at asserting dominance, they had happily fallen into line and were now licking his hands.

I wondered how much of Matt and Drew's behavior around women was due to their military training, and how much to their Christian upbringing. Certainly a lot of the devout Christians I had known suffered from a serious case of male over-confidence. And women totally bought into it and only felt comfortable around those kinds of men. As witnessed by Ruth and Naomi, who were more than smart enough to think for themselves, but apparently only felt safe around men who would tell them what to do. I thought some hard thoughts about the military, patriarchal religion, and male bonding, and how they all contributed to a society of rigid hierarchies and dominance struggles. Then I gave it up as a hopeless case, and went to make my printouts.

13

Making the printouts took longer than it should have, of course. There was a wait for a working computer, and then a wait for a working printer, and then the first, ostensibly working, printer turned out to be out of toner, and I had to wait while the unfortunate work-study on duty switched out the toner cartridge so that I could try again.

By the time I was done, I had gotten a text from Naomi.

Ruth hasn't answered any of my texts or calls, and she's not back in her room, she wrote. *I'm starting to get worried about her.*

She's almost certainly fine, but you might as well start asking around, I wrote back. *Has anyone else at the dorm seen her? Maybe she ate something that disagreed with her and has been spending the morning in the bathroom.*

I'll start asking around, Naomi replied. *Where else do you think we should look? I keep thinking about that girl on all the posters around town, the one who disappeared. And they say a girl was murdered here just this spring, too!*

I'm sure that's not what happened to Ruth, I assured her. It was true that Lauren Spierer had disappeared in 2011, and Hannah Wilson had been murdered just this past April. Missing and murdered students were not that too terribly uncommon in college towns. Normally, as in the case of those two girls, it happened after a hard night of partying, not when a student was supposed to be meeting with a professor.

What if there's a serial killer out there? Naomi texted.

It seems extremely unlikely that a serial killer would snatch someone out of the fourth floor of Ballantine Hall in broad daylight, I texted back. *The most likely explanation is what you already suggested yourself: her phone broke and she went off to get it fixed. Or she suddenly started feeling bad or twisted her knee or something, and is resting in the ladies' room somewhere. Why don't you go ask around the dorm, see if anyone's seen her, and I'll go do a sweep of Ballantine Hall.*

Okay. I guess that's the right place to start. Thanks, Professor!

No problem. I'm sure we'll find her soon. I'll be in touch, okay?

Are you up for some search and rescue? I texted Alex next. *Naomi's worried about Ruth.*

She's still missing? Okay. I'm still with Drew and Matt. Maybe they can help.

Five minutes later, all four of us met outside the Union. Alex looked vaguely annoyed. Drew and Matt looked worried.

"I haven't heard anything from her since last night," Matt said when I asked him. "We walked them back to the dorm—you can't be too careful here, you know? We heard about what happened to those other girls. Ruth was scared to walk around by herself at night because of it. She's always real careful like that. So we walked them back to Willkie, and that was the last we saw them. We were supposed to get together for supper tonight, and church tomorrow morning. We asked if they wanted to go get some lunch together today, but they said they had to study, and to be honest, so do we. The homework here is out of control...anyway, we thought they were supposed to be studying together all day today."

"Do you know where Ruth likes to study?" I asked.

Matt shrugged. "Mostly her dorm, I think. She didn't like being around other people too much if she could help it. She found just being in class exhausting."

"Wasn't she talking about going to the library?" Drew put in. "She wanted to check out some Russian novels or something, see if she could read something in Russian."

"Yeah, that's right. I think she said something about that. And she wanted to talk to her mom about something, and she said she couldn't do it in the dorm—it wasn't private enough."

"So maybe she went to the library," I said. "Could you two go check it out? Naomi is looking for her in Willkie. And I'll go look again in Ballantine."

"Sounds good," said Matt. Now that we had a plan, he was looking less worried. "And we'll text when we find her, okay?"

We exchanged texts in order to have each other's numbers, and then each set off our separate ways.

14

"**I**s this really worth it?" Alex asked, once we had separated from Drew and Matt and were heading back to Ballantine. "I mean, she's almost certainly off somewhere shacked up with some guy or nursing a hangover, right?"

"If it were someone else, I'd agree, but it sounds like Ruth isn't that kind of girl by temperament, and she's a Pentecostal, to boot."

"Yeah, well, so are Drew and Matt, and I'm pretty sure by what they said over coffee just now that they've had their fair share of one-night stands."

"Yeah, but they're men."

"I don't know how to respond to that," said Alex. "Especially since I don't know what you mean by it."

"Mainly what I meant was that there is very definitely a double standard about that kind of thing, especially amongst religious groups. No doubt Drew and Matt got plenty of lectures about maintaining their purity when they were teenagers, but no one would be surprised if they went off and sowed a few wild oats. And now they're, what—Rangers?"

"Rangers," confirmed Alex. "God help us all. They wanted to know if I was a SEAL, and I was all like, 'No, dudes, Cryptologic Warfare Officer, and then they started to get in my face again, so I had to play the Iraq vet card, which I fucking hate. Jesus! Special Forces! They're intolerable."

"Yeah. And unless I'm much mistaken, I don't think chastity and purity are a big part of that culture."

"That is not the impression I have, no."

"Whereas Naomi said that Ruth was still wearing a purity ring. She only took it off when she got here, because the other students made fun of it, but I saw it on the chain around her neck, next to her cross."

"What's a purity ring?" asked Alex.

"It's a ring you wear before getting married to signify your intention to remain a virgin until your wedding."

"Seriously?" Alex made a face. "That's...I don't know. Somehow that just seems gross to me. Like you're flaunting your business in everyone's face. It's like the opposite of modesty or something."

"Yeah," I said. "But it's a big deal in some circles, and apparently it meant a lot to Ruth."

"Even so. That doesn't mean she's not shacked up with someone right now. You know how it is: it's the ones who are most repressed who go the craziest when they finally decide to cut loose. I can state with a fair amount of confidence that Drew and Matt aren't eligible to wear purity rings anymore, and haven't been for a long time."

"Yeah, but like I said, they're men. The rules are different. And if Ruth were to, you know, decide now was the time to experiment with sex, I think she'd do it with Matt. He'd be perfect for it, actually. Safe enough with their shared religion, but also a comparative stranger, someone who might be able to get her to walk on the wild side and not spread tales back home. That's certainly what I'd do if I were her."

"Is that so." Alex gave me a sideways look. "You seem to have thought a lot about this."

"Certainly not about sleeping with Matt! Ugh! But I've known a lot of girls like Ruth, and that's how they tend to operate."

"Oh." Alex paused, and then said, "So, I've never asked, but now I'm curious: is *your* family religious? I mean, I know you're from the South. I just never got that vibe off you."

"Some of them are. Not my parents. They went the other direction and became full-blown hippies. But that meant that we were kind of in, for want of a better word, the alternative South, and that includes evangelicals and Mennonites and all those people as well as ultra-liberal hippies. We were all homeschooling together, if you see what I mean. So I know girls like Ruth. I'm not saying she wouldn't do something wild. But for her, 'doing something wild' would probably be running off and getting married without her parents' permission, not sleeping around."

"So maybe that's what she did," suggested Alex. "Maybe she eloped."

"It's certainly possible. But then why schedule a meeting with me? Why not skip that step, or elope afterwards?"

"Good point, although not one that's making me feel better about this."

"I know," I said. "Although I still think it's extremely unlikely she was abducted by a serial killer or anything like that. But let's do a quick pass through Ballantine in case she got food poisoning or tripped and smashed her phone and blew out her knee in the process or something like that and is now holed up in the restroom, not sure what to do."

We started in the deli-style cafeteria in the basement, and then moved up, looking in on all the computer labs and checking out the women's restrooms on each floor. By the time we got to the top, we were both out of breath and feeling like we'd gotten our climbing in for the day, but we'd seen no sign of Ruth.

"Anything from the others?" Alex asked as we rested against the wall outside the women's room on the eighth floor.

I checked my phone. "Nothing from Drew and Matt. Naomi is asking if we've found her. She hasn't found her anywhere in the dorm, and no one's seen her since this morning."

My phone *pinged*. "And now Drew and Matt are saying they couldn't find any sign of her in the library either. They didn't see her anywhere, and no one at any of the help or checkout desks has seen her. Matt tried to call her, but the call went straight to voicemail. He left a message, but she hasn't called back. I'm going to suggest that they go back and check their apartment, in case for some reason she decided to go there. Especially since it seems likely that when she left Ballantine, she was heading in that direction."

"I don't want to be unduly alarmist, but I have to be honest, I'm loving this less and less," said Alex. "I still think the most likely explanation is that she's shacked up somewhere with some hot dude, throwing off the shackles of her purity ring, or as you suggested, standing in front of a JP somewhere making her wedding vows, but I have to agree, it's a bit odd that she'd blow off a meeting with her professor *and* her new best friend without a word of warning. Does she have a favorite place to eat? Maybe she's there getting lunch right now."

"I'll ask."

I texted Naomi. She texted back immediately to say that Ruth's favorite place to eat was the Japanese restaurant near the Sample Gates on Indiana Avenue.

"Great," said Alex when I told him. "I hate to make it all about me, but I'm starving. Let's go grab some lunch there and ask if anyone's seen her."

"Sounds good. Maybe we'll even run into her there." I said it more hopefully than was warranted, but I was already tired of looking for Ruth, and being optimistic meant I could ignore the worry that was starting to spread from my gut to my head.

15

Naomi had texted me a picture of her and Ruth standing together in front of Beck Chapel, across from Ballantine Hall. When I showed the picture to the woman taking orders and operating the cash register at the Japanese restaurant, she recognized both girls and said they had come in for lunch on Thursday, but she hadn't seen either of them since then. She asked the cook working at the kitchen behind the bar if he had seen them, but he, dishing up our miso soup and salad with ginger dressing, shook his head and said something to the cashier in Japanese.

"We have been here since we opened this morning," the cashier told me. Her English was clear but careful. "We would have seen them if they had come here."

"Okay, thanks," I said. "If Ruth does come in, could you tell her that her friends are looking for her?"

"Of course." The woman gave me a professionally pleasant smile as she loaded our orders of sushi onto our trays. "Enjoy your meal."

The meal was delicious, especially for the price. I wished I could enjoy it more. I texted the lack of news to Naomi, who texted back that she was going to check in with Student Health to see if Ruth had ended up there.

"Good thinking," said Alex when I told him. "If she did sprain her ankle or something while tripping and falling and smashing her phone, she might have gone straight there. And I hate to be morbid, but if we're going to do this right, we should maybe check in with the local hospitals. She could have had a low blood sugar spell or something, blacked out, and someone could have called an ambulance and had her whisked off before she could tell anyone. And for another search avenue, do we know what kind of phone she had? What if she went to the store to get her phone fixed?"

"Naomi says she has an iPhone," I said, after another round of texting. "And it did have a cracked screen. She was thinking about having it fixed while she was here. Apparently there's an Apple store here in town, but it's a long walk from campus and Ruth was hoping to get a ride from someone out there. Matt offered to give her a ride out there this afternoon, but she said she wanted to wait until she got some money she was supposed to get from her parents later this month."

"Have Drew and Matt gotten back to you yet? Maybe she walked over to their apartment, hoping to get a ride out to the store."

I texted the question. Matt texted back a couple of minutes later that she wasn't there. When I asked him about the Apple store, he said he and Drew were going to go over there and see if she'd decided to walk over on her own.

And we'll check the mall too, he wrote. *She was talking of going shopping there.*

Sounds good, I texted. *Keep us posted.*

Naomi texted then to say that Student Health didn't have any record of Ruth there. She had gone ahead and called the police, who had told her that with Bloomington's history, they always took reports of absent students seriously, but three hours was much too soon to declare someone missing. They would keep an eye out for her, they said, and gave her a list of local hospitals to call if she wanted to.

"I'm going to let the program director know what's going on," I told Alex as we left the restaurant. "Just in case. And then...I can't think of what else to do."

"Letting the program director know seems like a good step," he said. "Other than that, you've done pretty much all you can for now. I'd say there's an excellent chance that Drew and Matt will find her making her way back from the Apple store."

"I still don't like Drew and Matt," I said.

"Who would? But do you think they're dangerous? To Ruth, that is."

"I imagine they're sure they have her best interests at heart. But my experience with very religious men is that they often act in what they think are women's best interests by doing terrible things."

"Fair point. You think they've got her locked away somewhere or something?"

"Honestly...probably not. Because then why were they walking around campus an hour later? Unless they're way savvier than I think they are."

"Yeah, exactly. I could see either of them committing a crime of passion, but something super-clever, not so much."

"Maybe they committed a crime of passion," I said, just to say something. "Maybe Matt stumbled in on Ruth and Drew fooling around in the classroom while she was waiting for me, and...I don't know."

"Under other circumstances, I could totally see that happening," said Alex. "But it was ten minutes, max, between when Naomi left Ruth and we showed up in the classroom. Killing people is gross. We would have found something nasty if she'd been strangled or bludgeoned to death there five minutes before we showed up."

"Yeah, I know. Maybe he just dragged her away?"

"Dragging people away is also messy. There wasn't any sign of a struggle, no screaming, nothing like that. And then how long a walk would it be back to their apartment?"

"At least a mile. But there's a parking lot in the back of Ballantine," I said.

"Okay. Let's say, just for the sake of speculation, that Drew and Matt have some kind of super-devious plan to kidnap Ruth, which they decided to implement not when they were walking her home from dinner last night, or driving her home from church tomorrow, but in the narrow window while she was waiting for you in her classroom, with other occupied classrooms on the same hall. There's a long walk from the classroom to the parking lot, right?"

"Yes. And down several flights of stairs, too."

"I'm sure, especially if they were working together, they could have overpowered her and carried her off. At least I hope that two Rangers could overpower an unarmed civilian, although since they're, you know, Army, I wouldn't hold my breath. But it would be risky. Very hard to avoid notice. And then why go taking me out for coffee an hour later?"

"I know," I said. "My personal antipathy towards them doesn't mean that they're guilty of anything other than behaving according to how they were raised. I'm going to email the program director about it, and then let's go back home. We've got other things we could and should be doing."

"Not to be heartless, but that sounds promising," said Alex.

16

I emailed Joan, the program director, about the situation. She wrote back to say that, while it was far too early to be concerned, she would send out a program-wide email asking everyone to keep an eye out for Ruth, and let her know as soon as she showed up.

By the time Alex and I had gotten to 10th Street, I'd gotten the program-wide email about Ruth, along with a personal email from Joan saying she'd also spoken with the police, who'd told her the same thing they'd told Naomi; namely, that it was far too early to declare Ruth missing, but, given Bloomington's history with disappearing students, they would keep an unofficial eye open. Joan said she would call Ruth's parents if she didn't show up by the evening.

I hate to be alarmist, she wrote. *But better safe than sorry. You've done all you can, so try to enjoy the rest of your weekend.*

I'll try, I wrote back, and filled Alex in on what was going on.

"She's right," he said. "You've done all you can. She'll probably turn up by suppertime, or at the latest for church tomorrow, mortified at all the trouble she's caused."

"Yeah, imagine if she just decided she wanted a couple of hours of peace and quiet, fell asleep in a carrel somewhere, and woke up to a massive search? Awkward!"

"Hardly the worst outcome, but yeah, super-awkward."

I didn't say what both of us knew, which was that Ruth had been a long way from any library carrels when she had last been seen, and it was very unlikely that she could have fallen asleep for long in an empty classroom. Even if for some reason she had moved to a different classroom between when Naomi had left her and I had shown up, the chairs were just not that comfy, and there had been plenty of activity, including me and Alex roaming up and down the hallways looking for her.

"You said she was shy, right?" said Alex, apparently sensing my thoughts and trying to come up with something comforting to say. "And Naomi said she wanted to meet with you to ask about going on a mission trip to Russia, but she was embarrassed about talking to any of the students or the other instructors about it? So she most likely lost her nerve, ran off before you showed up, and now she's too embarrassed to tell you or any of her friends what she did. For all we know, she's hiding out in Starbucks or something, trying to come up with the courage to go back and face everyone."

"Maybe," I said. "It's just so irresponsible."

"Yeah, but she's, what, like, twenty-two? She's probably not thinking about how we're all looking for her. All she's thinking about is her own embarrassment. Shy people can be incredibly self-centered that way, not that they'd admit that's what's going on."

"You sound like you're speaking from experience," I said.

"Me?" Alex grinned. "You may be surprised to hear it, but I was too much of a hothead to be shy. Nerdy and socially awkward, sure, but not shy."

"You? A hothead? You shock me," I said.

"Let me guess: You were always too busy standing up for the downtrodden and throwing yourself at injustice to be shy."

"How did you *know*?"

Alex glanced around, and, satisfied that the coast was clear, kissed me. "In case you haven't noticed, Rowena, I've been paying close attention to you since the day you came into that faculty meeting and sat down next to me. I thought my lucky day had come—if I could keep from throwing myself at you right there on the conference table, that is."

"That would have made that meeting a lot more interesting," I said. "Although I'm glad you waited until we got to know each other a little better before throwing yourself at me."

"Yeah. But anyway, some of my friends back in undergrad were painfully, horribly shy. No surprises, since I was in the Computer Science and Middle Eastern Studies programs. They would pull that kind of shit all the time. And I may have a time or two as well, but I got over it fast. There were always fights that needed fighting. Anyway. Super-shy people don't have a problem with flaking out on meetings. Their number-one concern is their own fear and awkwardness. They will totally fail to show up and not bother to so much as a send a text giving you a heads-up about their abrupt change in plans. And then if you ask them what happened, they get all defensive. Probably this Ruth of yours is socially aware enough to realize that she's done the wrong thing, but not sensible enough to fix the problem by sending a two-line text."

"You're making me feel better," I said.

"Yeah?"

"Yeah. I've certainly met plenty of people like that in Slavic Studies as well. And like you, I may have been like that a time or two as well, but as you said, there were always fights that needed fighting. No doubt you're right. I'm not going to worry about it anymore."

"So." We were approaching the house. The road was still empty of passers-by, so Alex took the opportunity to kiss me again. "Does that mean our original plan for passing the afternoon sloooowlly is still on?"

"It's your lucky day," I said.

17

After we had passed a good deal of the afternoon slowly, if with a fair expenditure of energy, I started to fret again.

"Are you checking your phone?" asked Alex. He was running his hand lazily through my hair while I rested my head on his chest, and he had switched from his setting of high-intensity concentration to his setting of almost boneless languor. Normally when that happened it was because he was tuning out his irritating surroundings, but right now he was still focused on me, just, for a change, completely relaxed.

"Just for a second." I opened my email app. "Oh jeez."

Alex's hand stilled on my hair. "What?"

"Still no sign of Ruth. So Joan—the program director—asked her mother if she'd heard from her, and now her mother's freaking out. Says this is totally unlike her and she's never done anything like this before and we have to find her."

"By we," said Alex, "you mean the police, I presume."

"They still haven't seen any sign of her. Joan checked. And it's too early for them to be out dragging all the local lakes and stuff. Joan wants to know if I have any ideas of places Ruth likes to hang out."

"And do you?"

I strained at my memories of the past week. "She hardly ever talked at all. But...yesterday we were talking about favorite restaurants, and she mentioned going to Mother Bear's Pizza and liking it. That's the only thing I can think of."

"Where's this Mother Bear's Pizza? Nearby?"

"It's on 3rd Street. On the other side of campus from where we are now. But not that far from Ballantine and Willkie, Ruth's dorm."

"You're not going to be happy until we go check it out, are you?"

"Do you mind?"

"Not at all. We can satisfy your curiosity and maybe pick up some pizza as well. I call that a win. But only on one condition."

"What's that?"

"We take my car. I'm old and worn out. I can't drag my ass across your mega-campus after the workout you just gave me. Call me a wimp if you will, but that's the sad truth."

"You weren't a wimp when it counted," I told him. "Let's go."

A quick shower and change later, and we squeezed into Alex's elderly car—"How are you going to get this thing to California?" I asked—shoving a random assortment of backpacks and book bags into the backseat, and navigated the grid of one-way streets from 12th Street to 3rd Street, which was more complicated than it sounds. We even found parking, which made me feel like luck was with us.

Luck appeared to desert us once we got into the restaurant and I showed the picture of Ruth on my phone to the girl taking our orders.

"She looks familiar," she said, her forehead wrinkling in a frown of half-recognition. "But I'm pretty sure I didn't see her today. I *think* I might have seen her come in a couple of days ago, but not since then."

"Okay. Do you think you could ask if anyone else has seen her?"

"I'll see," said the girl, sounding doubtful.

"Dead end," said Alex when we sat down at our table. "Hope the pizza's good, at least."

"It is," I promised. "As you're about to find out—oh, hey, Caitlyn."

"Rowena! Oh, wait, I should be calling you 'Doctor Halley' now, shouldn't I?"

"Technically, but in this case it seems a little silly. Caitlyn was my student my last year here in grad school," I explained to Alex.

"Nice to meet you," said Alex.

"Yeah, you too!" Caitlyn stared at him with unabashed curiosity. "Is this him?" she asked. "He doesn't have much of a Russian accent, does he?"

"Um," I said. "This is, uh, Alex. Who's an American."

"Oh! Ooops. I mean, she normally has Russian friends," Caitlyn said to Alex. "That's, uh, what I meant there about, um, anyway..."

"No worries," said Alex.

"Yeah, so, um...your pizzas are ready..."

"Really, don't worry about it," I said to Caitlyn as she deposited the pizzas on our table. "Alex—Doctor Miller—knows about my dark Russian past."

"Doctor Miller?" Relief broke out on Caitlyn's face like a sunrise, or some cliché like that, at the news that Alex was an academic too. "So, are you, like, colleagues, then?" In her mind, it was obvious, two PhDs couldn't possibly be engaged in any kind of relationship other than professional.

Alex tried and only partially succeeded in suppressing a grin. I could tell that he was remembering some of our more "collegial" activities today.

"Something like that," I said. "Hey, maybe they told you: we're looking for one of my students. No one's seen her today that we know of, and we're trying to track her down, make sure she's okay. We know she liked this place. Have you seen her? Here, let me show you her picture."

I showed her the picture of Ruth on my phone. Caitlyn frowned. "I remember her coming in a couple of days ago, I think," she said. "With a, um, another girl"—it was clear that Caitlyn felt uncomfortable saying "with a black girl" in case that was construed as racist—"that girl in the picture, in fact, I think. And two guys. Big guys, crew cuts."

"Yeah, that sounds like Ruth and her friends," I said. "But you haven't seen any of them since?"

Caitlyn started to shake her head. Then she paused. Then she shook her head, but doubtfully. "I don't *think* so," she said. "But...look, I gotta go, but I'll ask around, okay? Can you text me that picture?"

"Sure. Let me know if it sparks any memories in anyone, okay?"

"Sure thing, Doctor Halley!" Caitlyn grinned at that. "I know you said I don't have to, but it sounds so good, doesn't it? I think that's what I'll call you now. And I'll let you know if anyone remembers anything. Enjoy your pizza!"

18

"You know," said Alex, "I was prepared for a weekend of hardship out here in Bumfuck, Indiana—"

"What are you going to do, O snobby Yankee, when you come visit me in Georgia?" I interrupted.

"Let you be my wingwoman and native guide, I guess. *Anyway*, as I was saying before I was so rudely interrupted, this pizza is actually really good. In fact, everything I've eaten here so far has been really good."

"Insert obligatory sexual innuendo here," I said.

"Do I get to respond to the fact that you used the word 'insert'?"

"Do you really want to get in a dirty pun war with me?"

"Bring it on, baby, bring it on—aw shit, looks like your student's coming back. We'll have to take a rain check."

Caitlyn came back, leading another server behind her. "This is Sam," she said.

Sam, who was a girl, nodded uneasily. Sam, I could tell, did not like being dragged out to talk to a couple of professors.

"Sam thinks she might have seen that girl," Caitlyn informed me. "Today."

"When?" I asked.

Sam shuffled unhappily. "I'm not 100% sure it was her," she said. "I remember her coming in on Thursday, same as Caitlyn. Well, I remember who she was with. I remember the, you know, the other girl"—Sam also obviously didn't want to come out and say that she remembered Naomi because she was black, although it was very true that black students in Bloomington were few and far between, and would have stuck in anyone's memory—"and the guys"—Sam grinned at the memory—"and I kinda remember her, but she didn't stand out like the others, you know what I mean?"

"I know what you mean," I said. "But you think you saw her today?"

Sam nodded uncertainly. "I *think* so. I was walking down 3rd Street on my way to class this morning, and I passed a girl and two guys walking the other way. They were arguing, which is why I remembered them. I was running late for my ten o'clock class, so I didn't pay much attention, but they were arguing so much they almost ran into me, and I had to step aside to let them past. I thought the girl looked familiar. Then when Caitlyn here showed me her picture, I remembered the girl, and I think it might have been her."

"Do you remember the guys?" I asked. "Was it the same ones she was with on Thursday?"

Sam shook her head, but not with a lot of certainty. "I don't think so. But I wasn't really paying attention. It could have been. They were about the same height. But I don't think they were as hot as the guys she was with on Thursday. I woulda remembered that."

I did a mental eye roll. "Yes, the guys she was with on Thursday are memorable. Which way were they going?"

"Away from campus," Sam said promptly. "I was rushing to class, like I said, and they were walking really fast in the opposite direction, arguing. It was right before they woulda got to the coffee shop at the corner up by campus."

"Did you catch anything about what they were arguing about? Where they were going?"

Sam shook her head. "'Fraid not." She shuffled a little more. "So, can I, like, go now? Only I've got stuff to do, and I've told you all I know."

"Sure," I said. "And thanks a lot. You've been a big help."

Sam shrugged, like she wasn't sure about that and didn't care that much, and ducked off before we could detain her any further. Caitlyn gave me a bright smile and followed her off into the depths of the kitchen.

"Okay," said Alex. "If Sam is telling us the truth, then at least we know Ruth was still alive as of 10:00am this morning."

"You think she's lying?"

He shook his head. "I don't think she's lying. But her statement doesn't inspire a huge amount of confidence. She *may* have seen someone she'd seen only once before. And she can't identify the other people at all. They *may* have been Drew and Matt. Or maybe not."

"They were walking in the direction of Drew and Matt's apartment when Sam saw them."

"Really?"

"Yeah," I said. "I know where it is. It's a few more blocks down 3rd Street in the direction they were going."

"I bow to your superior knowledge. So what do you want to do about it?"

"I guess," I said, with a distinct lack of enthusiasm, "we need to talk to Drew and Matt again."

19

Still feeling a distinct lack of enthusiasm, I texted Matt to say that we'd found someone who claimed to have seen Ruth walking down 3rd Street this morning in the company of two men. Could it have been them?

No, for sure not, he texted back. *I told you: we haven't seen her since last night.*

They were walking in the direction of your apartment, I wrote.

Well, I don't know what to say, because it wasn't us.

I take it you still haven't heard from her? I texted. I could practically feel the offense Matt had taken at my suggestion rolling off the phone in waves. Maybe this would give him a chance to cool down.

No. Look—now I could feel his attempt to be conciliatory coming over the phone connection—*why don't we get together and share information and discuss strategy? You've obviously put a lot of effort into looking for her*—it was a good thing we were separated by several city blocks, or otherwise I would have been hard pressed not to do something unwise about the condescension that was dripping, entirely, I was sure, unconsciously, from his every word—*and it's great that you found someone who thinks they've seen her. We should figure out what to do next. The cops sure as hell aren't going to do anything.*

They're keeping an eye out for her, I wrote, instead of what I thought about men who treat female professors like they're mentally

60

handicapped toddlers who've finally figured out how to dress themselves.

Yeah, but they're not taking it seriously, are they? They think she's just another ho like those other girls who went missing, they're not going to bother searching until it's too late.

I exhaled sharply through my nose. Alex looked over at me. "What now?"

"Matt is a jerk. An insensitive, sexist jerk."

"Yeah. Want me to take over the comms?"

"No. He wants us to get together and pool information and strategies."

"That's not actually a bad idea," said Alex.

"I know it isn't. I'm just trying to overcome my innate distaste for having anything to do with him."

"I could do it. You wouldn't have to be involved."

"No. She's my student, and I'm the one who knows Bloomington. I need to take point on this. Plus, you're here as my guest. I can't let you do my dirty work."

"I appreciate the sentiment. Also, I'd sure as hell rather be with you than those two. What do they want to do?"

I checked my phone. "They're suggesting we meet at their apartment."

Alex made a face.

"It would be private and quiet. Also, I think Matt is pissed that I asked him if it was him with Ruth this morning. He says we can come search the place and see for ourselves that she's not there."

"I'm not loving this plan, but it's probably the best we've got," said Alex. "Let's go."

20

We took Alex's car from Mother Bear's to where Drew and Matt were sharing a sublet, a few blocks down the street. It had once been a nice apartment complex, with two-story buildings attractively faced with limestone around a central quad. But now it had straggly weeds instead of grass, trash overflowing from the dumpsters that were out in plain sight in the middle of the complex, and cheap cars parked in front of the units. So, like everywhere else in Bloomington.

The inside of the apartment was even less inspiring. It, too, had once been nice, but now the shag carpet was stained, the vertical blinds over the door to the patio were missing half their slats, the furniture was falling apart, and there was a big stain in the kitchen ceiling above the sink. At least it was neat. You could say a lot of bad things about the military, but it did teach people how not to be slobs.

"Feel free to search the place," said Matt when we came in. The expression on his face said he was still deeply pissed at the implication that he had had anything to do with Ruth's disappearance. Drew, who was standing next to him, was wearing a similar expression. "We've got nothing to hide."

"I can tell," I said. "I used to live in the apartment down the hall. I know that I can see everything except the en suite bathroom to the second bedroom from where I'm standing right here in the living room."

"Well, you can go check that out too, if you want to."

"I do, but not because I think you're hiding anyone or anything like that. I just really need to wash pizza grease off my hands."

"Oh." Matt looked fractionally less pissed. "Sure. It's through there."

I stepped through the bedroom and into the en suite bathroom whose layout I knew like the back of my hand, after living in an identical apartment for a year. Matt, I noted, kept his bathroom as neat as I kept mine, although he, like me, had been hampered in his quest for cleanliness by the crud growing on the walls and coming through the ceiling. There was a single bottle of generic shampoo in the shower, and a bar of plain soap in the soap dish on the sink. I eased open the door to the mirrored medicine cabinet above the sink as silently as I could. Toothbrush, toothpaste, a man's razor and shaving cream, a mostly full bottle of cheap cologne, and an unopened box of condoms, its packaging still bright and crisp from the store. I eased the door closed and rejoined the others in the living room.

21

"**L**ooks like you've got at least as much water damage here as my place did," I said, cautiously taking a seat on a rickety chair next to the equally rickety chair where Alex was gingerly perching. Drew and Matt were sitting on the couch, one on each side of the vaguely obscene-looking explosion of stuffing from a hole in the middle of the upholstery.

"Yeah. They advertised this as a luxury furnished apartment. Luxury my ass." Matt looked embarrassed. "Uh, sorry. I know I shouldn't talk like that. My mom'd wash my mouth out with soap if she heard me. It's just, you get used to it, you know, in the military."

"My brother's a career Marine," I said. "Sometimes I think he's constitutionally incapable of uttering a single sentence that doesn't have the word 'fuck' in it at least three times."

Matt and Drew both laughed. A bit uncomfortably, but they still laughed. Progress. Maybe they weren't such complete dickheads after all. Actually, I knew that they weren't dickheads, or any worse than usual. They just had been trained to act in a way that I found particularly irritating. Although it probably came naturally to them as well. But they might also be some of the best allies I could have in the search for Ruth. The same arrogant belief in their own moral rectitude and their right to tell other people what to do that made them so annoying could also keep them going when many other people would shrug their shoulders and say Ruth was none of their business.

"Naomi told me that you all belonged to the same church," I said. "That that was one of the things that brought you together."

"Yeah. Well..." Drew and Matt shared a look. "Not exactly the same church," Matt said. "I mean, yeah, we're all Pentecostals, but there are different branches of it. So we're, like, sort of from the same church, but not really."

"Naomi and I are both from the same branch of the church," Drew said. "Same as Matt. But Ruth's family..." Both men whistled.

"Even we think they're crazy," Matt said. "They're really into the speaking in tongues, shit—oh shit, sorry, I mean—anyway, speaking in tongues, even snake handling and shit like that. Ruth said her grandpa's hands were all swollen and scarred from all the times he'd been bitten. And he never went to the hospital or anything for it either."

"Fuck," said Alex. "Oops, sorry," he added. "I guess whatever floats your boat."

"Most of us don't do that shit anymore," Drew told him earnestly. "I mean, yeah, we believe that Jesus can heal, but we don't *believe* it, if you see what I'm saying. Like, I got all my shots and stuff, and when I broke my leg falling off my bike when I was kid, my dad took me in and got a cast for me. But Ruth's family is hardcore. Like, when her brother broke his arm, they just splinted it at home. Same with Ruth's finger. She showed me: it's crooked where she broke it and it didn't heal right."

Alex was making a face. "That sounds like child abuse," he said.

"Yeah, but so's drugging kids out of their fucking minds on Ritalin so they'll sit in classrooms all day, every day, and not flip the fuck out. So's having kids in schools where they could get shot dead at any moment. So's dressing little girls up like sluts and telling them it's 'empowering.' So's..."

"I get it," said Alex, before Drew could get any angrier. "I don't even disagree with you. A lot of the shit we do to kids these days is horrific, and I say this as a professional educator. I'd still get a broken bone set properly."

"Yeah." Drew nodded, calming down. "So would I. Or Naomi's family. But Ruth's family were, like I said, hardcore. So Ruth was having a hard time here. She kind of latched on to us as soon as Naomi introduced us. Not that Matt minded, did you, man?"

"No." Matt smiled briefly. "But it wasn't, like, you know, I didn't...I don't know..."

"You liked her a lot but your intentions were honorable," I interjected.

"Yeah." Matt gave me a look of surprise. "How'd you know?"

"I have my ways." *Like snooping through your medicine cabinet*, I thought but did not say. The cologne and the condoms had spoken so clearly to me of an innocent hopefulness that maybe Matt was embarrassed to admit to even to himself, let alone Drew and especially Alex. So I wasn't going to bring them up. "Women's intuition," I said instead. "I could tell right off the bat you really liked Ruth, and you wanted to treat her right."

"Yeah." Matt made an indeterminate sort of twitch. "I, uh, I mean, we'd only just met, but I could already tell that she had, like, promise, you know what I mean? Like, maybe"—he shrugged his shoulders, carefully not looking at either Drew or Alex—"maybe it could get, like, serious."

"Ruth seems like a very nice girl," I said encouragingly.

"Yeah, and she also, like, she needed, like, someone to look out for her, watch her back. She didn't know how to deal with, like, the kind of people she was meeting here."

"It's good that you two met so soon, then," I said.

Matt gave me a look. "I thought, no offense, professor, but that you, like, didn't like me." He looked over at Alex. "Either of you."

"I like Ruth," I said, although in truth Ruth had been such a nonentity in my class that "like" was much too strong a word for what I felt for her. "And I can see how you would be good for each other."

"Really?"

"Yes. I grew up in a very religious community. A lot of my friends were like Ruth. I can see how she'd feel a lot more comfortable around you than most of the other guys here."

"Oh." Matt sat back, digesting this unexpected vote of support.

"Anyway," said Drew, when it became apparent that Matt wasn't going to say anything more. "We don't know where Ruth is. And whoever it was she was with this morning, it wasn't us. I wish we could help you, professor, I really do, but frankly, we're outta ideas. You think those guys were, like...bad? You think they were planning to do something bad to Ruth?"

"I'm just reporting what I heard second-hand," I said. "I don't know who they are, or what they were doing. But it sounded like Ruth was walking with them more or less of her own free will. It sounded like she wasn't happy to be with them, but it didn't sound like she was being dragged away, either."

"Ruth's not the kind of girl who'd scream and shout and make a big fuss," Matt said. "She'd probably be polite to a serial killer, and offer to pray for him, or something."

"Yeah," said Drew. "Unfortunately."

"Ruth's mom says she doesn't know where she is," I said. "Do you have any contacts with her church? Maybe it was someone from there."

Drew and Matt shook their heads. "Like I said, not our branch," said Drew. "But we can ask around. A buddy of mine, the one who put me in touch with the church here, leads an inter-church youth group now. Maybe he'll know something."

"It's as good a place to start as any." I stood up. "Thanks for helping us. Hopefully by tomorrow morning there will be good news."

"Yeah," said Matt. "Because otherwise there'll be bad news."

Drew punched him in the arm. "Don't say that, man!"

"Someone has to," said Matt. "Goodnight, professor. And you, too, Professor Miller. Thanks for taking the time to talk to us today. And for looking for Ruth. Drew'll call his friend tonight, and we'll ask at church tomorrow if she doesn't show up before then."

"Maybe she will," I said. Matt shrugged doubtfully, and walked us to the door.

22

"I don't think they did it," said Alex, as soon as we got back into his car.

"You don't have to sound so glum about it."

"It would just be easy if it turned out they'd...I don't know. I don't want anything bad to have happened to her. But if they'd convinced her to throw off her purity ring and have a wild threesome or something, it would solve everything tidily, and I wouldn't feel so bad for all of them. Which I'm not enjoying, because I don't actually like any of them. Well, I don't like Drew and Matt, and I feel sorry for Ruth, and think that she's complicit in her own oppression, or something."

"I know," I said. "And she is. But this is why she probably feels more comfortable with Matt than with any of the other men here. Because they'd all feel sorry for her, but he respects her for who she already is."

"Makes sense. But seriously? Snake handling?"

"It's still a thing."

Alex cut a sideways glance at me as we waited at the light to turn onto 3rd Street. "Did you ever do it? Or see anyone else do it?"

"What? No. My parents were very much against that kind of thing. We were the godless hippies. But because we were part of the counterculture, we brushed shoulders with that aspect of it as well, like I said."

"The sad thing is, I think you may have had a better childhood than I did. I think *Ruth* may have had a better childhood than I did. Snake handling doesn't sound so bad compared with upper-middle-class suburban tedium. At least you got to live a little. And compared with modern psychiatric drugs, snake venom seems pretty benign. If it's gonna kill you, it'll kill you quickly."

"I know," I said. "And I think you're right. Oh, wow." I looked at my phone. "Ruth's mom wants me to call her."

"Does she say why?"

"Nope."

"Well, give her a call. The suspense is killing me."

"I'll wait till we get home. You've got to—no, oops, see, the street becomes one-way. Turn there. Yeah, right there. And then again there."

"Where *are* we?" asked Alex. "It looks like we're in the middle of a fucking forest."

"It's just campus. Now turn right at the intersection up ahead. And then take a left there. Now we're back on 10th Street."

"Thank God. Civilization. For a moment I thought we were going to spend the next forty years wandering through the woods or something."

"O ye of little faith. Take a right up there, and then the house will be two blocks down, on the left."

I started to call Ruth's mom as soon as we pulled up to my place, but had to abort the call before she picked up because a train chose that moment to go by on the tracks just behind the house.

"Does that happen often?" Alex asked, once we could hear each other again.

"This is Indiana. Train capital of the nation, or at least that's what it feels like. We're lucky this track only gets used a few times a week. A friend of mine works in Terre Haute, and she gets trains by her house at least five times a night."

"Note to self: do not accept job in Terre Haute."

"That's what she said. But that was the only job she could get."

Alex made a face. "That's too depressing to contemplate."

"You're a Yankee *and* a member of the coastal elite," I said. "Good thing you're cute."

"Under other circumstances I would be thrilled to hear you think I'm cute. But right now I just really want to hear what Ruth's mom has to say."

"Me too. Trying again."

23

Ruth's mom picked up on the second ring. "Doctor Halley?" Her voice was shrill. "Did you just call?"

"Yeah, sorry about that. I was out when I got your call, and it took me a little while to find a quiet place to call you back. Have you heard anything from Ruth?"

"No. No, I haven't." Her voice got even shriller. "This isn't like her at all! I've just spent the past two hours trying to get ahold of the chief of police in Bloomington, but they keep pushing me off, telling me she's probably off with a boyfriend or something! Ruth's not that kind of girl, I keep trying to tell them that, but they just won't listen! As far as they're concerned, every girl is just some, some *slut*"—I could tell that Ruth's mom wasn't used to saying words like that, and she pronounced it like it hurt her mouth on the way out—"and they won't do anything until at least tomorrow! What if tomorrow is too late? What if she's already..." Her voice choked off in a kind of gulping noise that wasn't quite a sob, but wasn't quite not a sob, before she could get the word "dead" out.

"I know," I said. "That's why we're already out looking for her."

"I know, and I thank you for it, and I know God is helping you find her. I talked to that woman—Joan, is it?—who runs your program, and she said you were the one who told her about what was going on with Ruth, and you'd been out looking for her, and I knew I just had to pray for you. So when I haven't been on the phone to those...those...I know

I should pray for them too, but I just can't right now, they were so rude to me...anyway, I've been praying for you real hard all afternoon, hoping you'll find her. Have you heard anything?"

"I just talked to someone who thinks she saw Ruth this morning. It would have been about the time she didn't show up for her meeting with me."

"Oh, thank the Lord. Who saw her? What was she doing?"

"It was a student here, who also works at a restaurant Ruth'd been to a couple of times. She passed Ruth on the street. She was walking away from our classroom, and she was with two men."

"Oh Lord! Was it..." Ruth's mom lowered her voice. "I heard she'd taken up with a *man*. Already! And she'd been going out with him *and* his friend. Is that true? Was it him?"

"It is true that she and her friend Naomi"—"I don't like what I've been hearing about this Naomi," Ruth's mom interjected—"had made friends with a couple of students in the Arabic program. But I'm pretty sure it wasn't them with Ruth this morning. I just talked to them, and they say it wasn't them."

"They could be lying!"

"Yes, but I also ran into them on the other side of campus a little bit later, and Ruth wasn't with them. So it seems unlikely that it was them. And they've been helping us look for her."

"Maybe to throw you off the scent!"

"Maybe," I said. "But I don't get that feeling from them. I think they're nice guys."

Off to the side, Alex choked and coughed. I kept my face perfectly smooth to avoid joining him.

"Well," said Ruth's mom. "Well...that's what Ruth said too, actually. She said she'd found a nice church-going boy here, where she'd least expected it. She called us up, oh, Thursday I think it was, all excited about it. I could feel her practically glowing about it, even over the phone."

I tried, and failed, to imagine Ruth glowing. "That's lovely," I said.

"I know. She said he wasn't from our church, but he was from *a* church, and that was better than nothing. And she's almost twenty-three. I've been worried about her, you know, finding a man in time...but now it sounds like she might have found one, only to disappear. Do you think"—Ruth's mom's voice took on a hopeful tone—"they might have run off together? I know I shouldn't encourage that kind of behavior, but...that's how *I* got married, after all. I ran away when I was seventeen, just as soon as I was old enough. I climbed out the window on my seventeenth birthday and met Luke—my husband—in his pickup around the corner...anyway. It seemed romantic when I did it. Now I think about what it put my parents through...but Ruthie grew up on that story, so maybe that's what she did too."

"I'd like to think so," I said. "But I was just at the apartment of her...of the man she was talking about, and I didn't see any sign of her."

"Oh. Well. I don't want to say this about my own daughter, but, um, could it have been a different man?"

"You mean could she have been telling you about a different man than the one I know about? I suppose. Do you think that's likely?"

"No," said Ruth's mom. "She was shy enough around men as it was. I can't imagine her going out with one and running off with another in the same week."

"Yeah," I said. "That's what I thought. Do you know of any friends she might have gone to? Back home, I mean."

"I've already called her friends here. Although..." Ruth's mom sucked in a breath. "There's always Aaron, our pastor's son. He was more friends with Mark, Ruth's brother, than with Ruth, but I think they may have, well, for a bit there it looked there might be something between them, but then...Aaron, he, well, he got into a bit of trouble. You know what they say about preachers' sons. We had to break off contact with him, and make sure Ruth and Mark did too. Although I always got the feeling that Ruthie kept in touch with him behind our backs. So maybe...if she was thinking about doing something wild...I'll give his mother a call, see if I can track him down. Actually," Ruth's mom's voice sounded stronger, "that seems the most likely thing, doesn't it? Now that I think of it, I think he lives somewhere not too far from Bloomington. Maybe she ran into him, and he talked her into going off with him. He always was thoughtless like that. I'll call his mother right now, and then I'll call him. Maybe by the time my husband gets home tomorrow—he left on a business trip first thing this morning...traveling on the Sabbath, I don't know what he's thinking—it'll all be straightened out."

"I hope so," I said. "That sounds like a good plan."

"I'm sure that's what happened," said Ruth's mom. "I knew Jesus would show me the way. Thanks for talking to me, Professor Halley, and I'll call you tomorrow to let you know that Ruth's okay."

24

I didn't hear back from Ruth's mom that evening, which I hoped was a good sign. I tried not to worry about it too much that night, although after a midnight train blew through and woke me up, I spent two hours lying awake and stressing about that and myriad other things, until Alex woke up too and said if we were going to be up in the middle of the night, we should take advantage of the situation and not waste it fretting.

There was still no news when I got up the next morning. I texted Naomi, filling her in on my conversation with Ruth's mom and asking if she'd heard anything.

Not yet :(she wrote back. *Going to church now. Maybe we'll hear something there.*

Let me know if you do! I replied.

"Anything?" asked Alex when I put down my phone.

I shook my head. "I haven't heard anything from her mom, and Naomi hasn't heard anything either."

"It'll be okay," said Alex.

"You don't know that."

"You're right. I don't. Maybe it *won't* be okay. Sometimes it isn't. But you're doing all the right things. The rest is out of your control."

"I know," I said. "I just hate it."

"I know you do. But it wouldn't surprise me at all if her mother *did* find her last night, and just hasn't bothered to let you know. You're a stranger to her; she probably didn't think of it, or didn't want to disturb you late at night or on a Sunday morning."

"Probably," I said. "In any case, you're right: it's out of my control now. What do you want for breakfast? Do you like bagels?"

"I don't hate them. What did you have in mind?"

"Let's go mosey on down to Bloomington Bagel Company. And maybe we'll get lucky and run into Ruth or something there too."

"We're more likely to run into her there than here," said Alex. "And not to be a selfish pig, but I'm starving. Let me just shave—and can I say, I'd forgotten what a pain in the ass this shaving every day is—and I'll be good to go."

Shaving might be a pain in the ass, but Alex looked good freshly shaven, which I told him twice on the way to the bagel shop.

"Shit," he said. "You're starting to make me feel like you didn't actually find me attractive before."

"I found you attractive. But this is new and exciting."

"I like the sound of that. Is that Naomi coming out of there?"

Naomi looked up just as Alex said her name. "Oh, hi, Professor!" she said. "I'm just grabbing some bagels on the way to church." She held up a bulging paper bag. "Drew and Matt are picking me up and asked me to get something we could eat in the car on the way over. I got a ton because I know they eat a lot. I never had a brother or anything, so I didn't know how much guys could eat till I started hanging out with them. But I guess those two run it all off."

"Yeah," I said. "Any news?"

She shook her head. "No. We're going to ask the church to pray for us and Ruth. I suppose you think that's silly, don't you?"

"No," I said, only semi-lying. "I think in times like this, you might as well do all you can."

"Yeah." She looked at the bulging paper bag. "I can't help but feel it's sinful to be eating while Ruth could be, I don't know, lost or hungry or something."

"Maybe she's fine," I said. "Maybe her mom was right, and she just hooked up with an old friend and forgot to tell us about it."

"That's pretty inconsiderate of her not to tell us," said Naomi. "But I'd rather be mad at her for being inconsiderate than be sad because...well, anyway. There's Drew's car. Let me know if you hear anything, Professor Halley."

"I will," I promised.

25

Alex and I ordered and sat down in the corner, watching as a steady stream of people, many of them students in the program, went in and out. None of them were Ruth.

I was finishing up my first bagel and contemplating my second when Jen and Tracy, two students from my group, came in.

"Oh, hi, Professor Halley!" called Tracy. Both girls made a detour to come over and say hello and tell me that they were about to go do their homework, they really were, and it would definitely be ready by Monday.

"Good," I said. "By the way, have you seen Ruth?"

Jen wrinkled up her forehead. "Who's Ruth?"

"Sits in the back? Next to Naomi?"

"Oh." Jen and Tracy shared a glance. "Yeah. She doesn't talk much, does she? So her name's Ruth?"

"Yeah," I said. "And she's gone missing."

Jen and Tracy did identical gasps. "Missing!" exclaimed Jen. "I know we got an email saying the program was looking for her, but that was, like, yesterday. I figured she'd shown up already. Missing? You don't think...you don't think something bad's happened to her, like with those other girls?"

"We hope not," I said. "But we're asking everyone to keep an eye out for her, in any case."

"I haven't seen her since class on Friday, Professor," said Jen.

"Yeah, me neither...wait," said Tracy. "Wait, wait, wait! Stop everything! I, like, I think I might've seen her yesterday. No, wait, I'm *sure* I saw her yesterday! I was running to grab an iced coffee at that coffee place on 3rd Street, you know, right before you get to campus, and I *swear* I saw Ruth! She was walking away from campus, arguing with two men. Or at least I guess she was arguing because she looked, like, pretty mad. I didn't recognize her at first because she, like, sits behind me, and I'd never heard her say anything in class or anything, and she'd certainly never argued or done anything like that, but now that I think about it, I'm sure it was her!" Tracy's eyes were round with excitement. "Do you think I was the last person to see her? Were those her kidnappers?"

"Trace!" Jen gave her a hard nudge in the side. "That's hardly appropriate."

"Yeah." Tracy tried to arrange her face into an expression more fitting for the news that she might have witnessed the kidnapping of a fellow student. "Yeah, um, well, should I, like, go to the police or something?" she asked me.

"It wouldn't hurt to give them a call," I said. "I don't know how seriously they'll take you, but it's good to have a record of this kind of stuff. Did you recognize the men?"

Tracy shook her head. "I only got a glance at 'em, but I'm pretty sure I'd never seen 'em before. But they stood in front of the coffee shop and argued for a while before all getting in the same car and driving away. Didn't look Ruth was being forced into anything. I mean, the girl working the register and I both saw 'em, we were both watching 'em 'cause it was kind of concerning, you know what I mean? An argument like that. But it looked like Ruth got in the car of her own free will. I remember the girl working the register saying something about it, even. She made some kind of joke about how for a minute there she'd thought she was gonna have to call the police, but then everything'd blown over."

"Do you remember what the car looked like?" I asked.

Tracy shrugged. "I think it was red," she said. "Not super old, but not super new, either. Just an ordinary car. I don't really pay much attention to cars."

"Yeah," I said. "I'd give the police a call and let them know about it, just in case."

"Oh boy!" Tracy's eyes went round with excitement once again. "I've never been a witness to a crime before! I've never had to give a statement to the police! This'll be, like, a whole new life experience!"

"It probably won't be as fun as you think it will be," I warned her, but she and Jen were already off, searching for the address of the police station on their phones so they could give their statements in person and maybe "Meet some hot officers" in the process.

26

"I feel stupid," I said to Alex when they were gone. "I didn't even think of checking out the other businesses on 3rd Street, asking if anyone had seen Ruth."

"I think you can be forgiven," Alex said. "Seeing as how you're not a trained investigator, and it's not really your problem anyway. And," he added before I could voice my objections, "you just found out about Ruth being on 3rd Street last night. How much door-to-door could you realistically get done on a Saturday night?"

"Would you mind very much if we go ask at the coffee shop? Maybe the same girl will be there, and she'll have something to add."

"I don't mind. On one condition. No, two. No, three."

"Oh?" I raised a brow at him. "Is this how it's going to be now? You're getting awfully demanding."

Alex tried and failed to stifle a grin. "You haven't seen the half of it, sweetheart. So, condition one: finish that bagel, or give it to me."

I pretended to snatch my second bagel away from him. "Get your own bagel! This one's *mine*."

"Hungry this morning, are we?"

"I need to keep up my strength. I had a busy night. *Someone* couldn't let me sleep."

Alex failed to stifle another grin. "And here I was thinking I was the one getting worked into the ground by your insatiable demands. Okay. The bagel is yours."

"I'm glad you recognize that. What's your second condition?"

"My second...oh, yeah." Alex pulled himself away from his thoughts of last night with a visible effort. "My second condition is that we drive over to the coffee shop rather than walk. You may enjoy going on a ten-mile forced march every time you cross campus, but I don't."

"Okay," I said. "I guess we can cater to the East Coast guest's weakness."

"Thank you for being so understanding. Especially since after last night, I don't think I've got any strength left at all."

"I hope you have *some* strength left."

"Well." He quirked an eyebrow at me. "I might be able to summon up some later."

"That's good. What's your third condition?"

"Just that you don't get too caught up in this, Rowena. I mean, either it's nothing, just a simple misunderstanding, or it's...something really bad. Either way, you don't want to get too caught up in it."

"I know," I said. "And I won't. But I won't be able to rest easy until I find out where Ruth is, or at least until we go and ask at the coffee shop."

"I know. And frankly, me neither. You think they're open yet?"

I checked my phone. "They should be. It's after nine. You ready to go?"

Alex took a piece of bagel off my plate and ate it. "I am now," he said.

27

After I had slapped Alex's hand, threatened to steal his coffee if that was how he was going to behave, and promised dire retributions for any further attempts on my food, we left the bagel shop, walked home—flirting and cutting up like teenagers all the way—got into his car, and navigated the one-way roads to the coffee shop on 3rd Street.

"Looks like it's open," Alex said as we pulled up. "Thank goodness. I can get my caffeine levels topped up after you demanded half my last cup of coffee as tribute."

"You offered it of your own free will."

"What can I say. I'm a sucker for women with black hair and blue eyes. I'm like putty in their hands."

"I was hoping for something a little firmer in my hands—oh, hi, Elspeth."

Elspeth, one of my students, choked out a "Hi, Professor" before pushing past us out of the coffee shop and joining two more students in a car parked next to Alex's. Before they got the doors closed, I heard the whole carful of students explode in wild mirth.

"Great," I said. "By tomorrow morning I'm going to have a reputation throughout the whole program as a sex-crazed nymphomaniac."

"And very deservedly so," said Alex. "Thank God. I wouldn't have you any other way."

"The desire to respond to that with another double entendre is strong, but I'll delay my gratification until after we question our latest subject."

"If she's here," said Alex. "Why don't I ask, since I'm planning to order coffee anyway."

The girl working the counter and cash register was a very perky blonde with a name tag that read "Brittany." When Alex asked, after he had sufficiently impressed her by requesting a large black coffee with no sugar—"Whoa, I don't know hardly anyone who drinks it like that!" she exclaimed on hearing his order—if she had been working there the previous morning, she told him cheerfully that yep, she worked there pretty much every morning.

"That's great," said Alex. "Do you happen to remember seeing a young woman who was arguing with two men and then got in their car?"

"Why?" asked Brittany. She gave Alex a look of suspicion, that morphed into one of titillated speculation. "Are you from the police? Did something bad happen to her?"

"Just a friend," said Alex. "And we don't think anything bad's happened to her, but we haven't heard from her and we just want to make sure she's okay."

"You look like you're from the police," said Brittany, now giving Alex a frank appraisal. "Ex-military, right?"

"Um, yeah," said Alex, looking less than thrilled at the turn the conversation was taking.

"I can always tell!" said Brittany. "I do like a man in uniform!" She emitted a throaty bedroom giggle that made even me, an unrepentantly straight woman, want to shudder and fan my face.

"I haven't worn a uniform in a long time," said Alex, looking even less thrilled at where this was going.

"Too bad." Brittany sighed. "I bet you'd look *great* in it. But you're plainclothes now, am I right?"

"Something like that," I put in before Alex could ruin things by telling the truth. "But right now we're here on a side trip, on our own time, to try to find out where Ruth is. The girl who got in the car with the two men yesterday morning. Do you remember her? Do you remember anything about the encounter?"

"I remember seeing it," said Brittany. She didn't favor me with a throaty bedroom giggle. More like an annoyed frown. "They came walking down 3rd Street from the direction of campus. They weren't exactly shouting at each other, but they weren't happy to be talking to each other, either, you know what I mean? They stood outside the car talking—arguing—for a minute or two, and then they all got in the car and drove away. I remember it 'cause I remember the car was parked here when I showed up to open, and I was thinking I might have to call and get it towed away. You're not allowed to park here unless you're a customer. And then they showed up and I thought I might have to call the police to come deal with 'em, they were arguing so hard. Not shouting, you know, just—you could tell they were angry with each other. Real angry. But instead of starting to hit each other or anything like that, they all got in the car and drove away."

"That's very helpful," said Alex. "Do you remember anything else about them? What did the men look like?"

Brittany gave him a warm look. "They weren't good-looking at all," she said. *Unlike you*, her look said. Oh God. If she kept this up I was going to have a hard time not giving her a slap.

"How old were they?" Alex asked. "Were they white? Black? Hispanic? Do you remember anything about their clothes? Their hair?"

"One was old," said Brittany. "Like forty at least. The other was younger, more like my age. They were white. Their hair and clothes were just...hair and clothes."

"Short hair? Long hair? Any noticeable scars? Tattoos? Jewelry?"

"Short hair," said Brittany. She had stopped flirting with Alex, and her face was now withdrawn, remembering the scene. "No scars or tattoos that I could see. I didn't notice any jewelry on the men, but the girl was wearing a necklace. I remember it because the older man pulled it out from under her shirt and shook it in her face. It looked"—she frowned in concentration—"like maybe it was a cross. Or a ring? Like maybe a cross *and* a ring?"

"That's right," I said.

"Really? Anyway, that's when I thought I was going to have to call the police, but as soon as he did that, the girl stopped arguing with him and got in the car."

"What do you remember about the car?" asked Alex.

Brittany shrugged. "I don't notice cars much. It was red."

"New? Old? Dirty? Clean? Four-door or two-door? Hatchback or sedan?"

"Well, when you put it like that...um, not real new, but not real old either. Clean, but not like it'd just gone through the car wash. It was, um, a four-door sedan. Just, you know, a car. I remember thinking it looked like my mom's."

"What kind of car does your mom drive?" asked Alex.

Brittany screwed up her face. "Um, I think it's a...Yaris? Does that sound right? Is that a kind of car?"

"It is," said Alex. "I'm going to show you a picture of a red four-door Yaris sedan. Just a second."

He pulled up a picture on his phone and showed it to Brittany.

"That's definitely my mom's car," she said. "And it sure looks like the car they got into, too, but I can't be sure. It was either that or something an awful lot like that, though."

"Did you see the plate?" Alex asked.

"Um...I think so? But I don't remember it."

"Was it an Indiana plate?" asked Alex.

"Oh. Um"—Brittany wrinkled her nose in concentration—"yeah. Yeah, it was an Indiana plate. But I don't remember the number."

"That's not surprising," said Alex. "Do you remember any of the letter or number combinations on it? Like," he added, when Brittany looked confused, "did any of them spark any special thoughts in you, or have any special meaning? Like MAD or DAM or something like that."

"Oh! Oh yeah! The plate had"—she giggled again—"L-I-K in it. LIK. I remember thinking that was pretty funny."

"That's extremely helpful," said Alex. "You've been very helpful, Brittany."

"Do you want my number?" she asked hopefully. "So that you can, like, ask me more questions?"

"That would be great," I said, stopping Alex from turning her down—or accepting her. I wasn't sure which would annoy me more.

"Oh. Yeah." Brittany wasn't nearly as happy about giving her number to me, but she did it anyway, telling Alex pointedly as she did so to give her a call anytime, for any reason. And with that, we were on our way.

28

"Good interrogating," I said, once Alex and I were back in his car. "I didn't know you had it in you."

"Yeah." He didn't look pleased at the compliment. In fact, he looked unusually grim, with stress-lines crinkling around his eyes, making him look almost forty, his actual age. I couldn't tell if it was from the encounter with Brittany, or caffeine withdrawal.

"Have some coffee," I said.

"What?" He looked down at the giant coffee cup he was still holding. "Yeah, good idea." He took a long draw of coffee. "Elixir of the gods," he said.

"Yeah. Anyway, good interrogating. You got all kinds of information she didn't even know she had."

"Yeah. And I didn't even have to resort to torture." He said it like it was supposed to be a joke, but he didn't look at all like laughing.

"Always a good thing," I said lightly. "But I don't know what we're going to do with this information. Unless you have the ability to hack into the BMV and search for cars."

"BMV?"

"What they call the DMV in Indiana."

"Oh. Yeah." Alex took another swallow of coffee and visibly pulled himself together. "I don't," he said. "Unfortunately. The way I see it, we have two options."

"Which are?"

"We can go to the police and tell them what we just found out, and get told to stop worrying and stay out of police business."

"What's option two?"

"Well, we know the car didn't belong to Drew, so we can cross them off the list. Drew was driving a blue Ford Focus with Ohio plates when he came to pick up Naomi this morning. Even someone with complete car blindness wouldn't mix up a blue car with a red one, and we have two witnesses independently corroborating the red car story. And people tend to recognize their own state's plates."

"Great," I said. "So what do we do with that info?"

"I'd suggest calling Ruth's mom and asking her if the car sounds familiar. Maybe it belongs to this Aaron dude she was talking about last night. Maybe the two men were the pastor and his son. She said Aaron was local, right? Like near Bloomington? He would have Indiana plates, then."

"True." I checked the time. "It's almost ten o'clock. She might be in church already."

"Maybe. Or she might not, or she might have her phone on, waiting to hear from Ruth or us."

"True. I'll give her a call."

I dialed from where we were sitting, hoping Brittany wouldn't run us off for being parked in front of the coffee shop when technically we were no longer customers. Ruth's mom picked up on the second ring.

"Hello?" she said breathlessly. "Ruthie?"

"I'm sorry," I said. "It's Rowena Halley, Ruth's instructor."

"Oh. Oh, okay. Have you heard anything?"

"We haven't heard anything from Ruth, but we wanted to check in with you, ask you about a few things. Did you speak with Aaron?"

"Yes. Yes, I did. And he said he's going to call you today. But he didn't know where she was. He hadn't heard from her for months, he said."

"*Ask her about the car*," Alex whispered in my ear.

"Of course I'll be happy to talk to him," I said into the phone. "I hope he calls soon. And we just talked to someone who saw Ruth get into a car with two men and drive off yesterday."

"Oh Lord!" cried Ruth's mom.

"She was okay when she was last seen," I said. "She seemed to get into the car of her own free will. It sounds like she might have known the men. We have a description of the car, and we were wondering if it sounded familiar."

"Okay," said Ruth's mom. "Although I wish my husband were here to hear this. He's much better with cars than I am. But he's not back from his business trip yet. Go ahead and describe it to me, and I'll see if I recognize it."

"I'm going to pass you over to a colleague of mine." I handed the phone over to Alex, who grimaced as he took it, but sounded authoritative and professional as he said, "Mrs. Brown? This is Doctor Miller. Thanks for agreeing to speak with us."

"Anything, if it will help get my Ruthie back," said Ruth's mom.

"It sounds like she was fine as of yesterday morning, which is a good sign," said Alex, still speaking with official-sounding authority. "She was with two men, one about her age, the other older. They all got into a red four-door sedan, possibly a Toyota Yaris, with Indiana plates. The witness got a partial plate number: L-I-K. Does that sound familiar? Do you know what kind of car Aaron drives?"

"A red four-door Yaris?" said Ruth's mom. She sounded faint, almost sick. "With Indiana plates?"

"That's right," said Alex. "Do you know if that's Aaron's car?"

"I...I don't know. I don't...maybe. It could be. I...I have to go now. Thanks. Thanks for helping out so much. I gotta go." She hung up the phone before Alex could say anything else.

"That's weird," I said.

"Yeah," said Alex. "Like maybe she recognized the car and didn't want to talk about it."

"Yeah. Maybe it belonged to Aaron and she didn't want us to know for some reason?"

"Maybe," said Alex. "But it just seems..."

Before he could finish saying what it seemed, my phone started to ring. An 812 number, so local.

"Hello?" I answered.

"Hi," said a male voice on the other end. "It's, uh, Aaron. Calling about Ruth."

29

"Hi Aaron," I said. "Thanks for calling."

"Yeah. Um, of course. I, uh, heard about what happened to Ruthie. She's, um, missing?"

"Yeah," I said. "So you haven't heard from her?"

"Nuh-uh. Not for weeks. Sounds really weird, though. Not like Ruthie at all."

"That's what we all think. Can you think of anywhere she might have gone? Anyone she might be with?"

"I'd like to think if she were in trouble, she'd come to me," said Aaron.

"That's what her mom said. Do you think she might be in trouble, then?"

I could hear Aaron shrug over the phone. "Why else would she run off?"

"What kind of trouble do you think would make her run off?" I asked.

"Uh, well, you know..."

I waited.

"I guess if she were, you know, like, pregnant or something," Aaron said in a rush.

"You think she'd run off in that case?" I asked. "Without even telling the father?"

"Maybe she told him and he told her he didn't want to have anything to do with it," said Aaron. "Or told her to get an abortion. She's pretty, you know, hardcore pro-life."

"Uh-huh," I said. "I'm sure. She was last seen in the company of two men; one about her age, one older. They all got into a red car with Indiana plates. Do you have any idea who they might be? Where they might have been going?"

"Nuh-uh," said Aaron. "But I don't really, like, mix with that crowd anymore. I'm kinda, like, not really welcome there anymore. Ruthie was the only one who didn't turn her back on me—but we haven't really been close in a while, either."

"If she were in trouble, who *do* you think she'd turn to?" I asked.

"Her mom?"

"Other than her mom."

"Um...definitely not her dad. He's, like, pretty scary. I mean, not really. He wouldn't do nothing *bad* or nothing like that, but...he's not like the kinda guy you'd go to if you were in trouble."

"Uh-huh?" I said.

"But...I dunno, she might go to Mark. Her brother."

"Are they close?"

"I mean, they're brother and sister. Who else is she gonna go to? Especially since he's in Indiana."

"He is?"

"Yeah. The family's in Illinois, you know, but they've got a business in Indiana. They import leather goods and stuff from Mexico, and they got a warehouse outside of Martinsville, at Ruthie's grandparents' old farm. They got the land for free, barns, all that kinda stuff, so they went ahead and set up their warehouse there, and Mark lives out there now, manages the warehouse."

"Have you talked to Mark recently?" I asked. "Do you think he knows anything about where Ruth is? Seems like she would have gone to him, if he's in Martinsville." Martinsville was a small town halfway between Bloomington and Indianapolis.

"Nah, I haven't talked to him. He and I haven't spoken in a while. Not since I left home and came out here, actually, which is funny, 'cause I'm just down the road. But I think I've got his number around somewhere, if you wanna talk to him."

"Um, sure," I said.

"Just a second."

I heard Aaron put down the phone and rummage around for a while. "You ready?" he asked, coming back on the line. "I got the address for the warehouse as well. You want that too?"

"Yeah, go ahead."

Aaron read me Mark's number and the warehouse address. I thanked him and asked him if he could think of anything else.

"Just try and find her," he said. "She's the best of 'em, of that family, and I hate to think of anything happening to her. The rest of 'em are real pills, but Ruthie was always decent, even when she didn't have to be. I hope nothing's happened to her."

"Me too," I said.

30

After I hung up, I filled Alex in on the conversation.

"What do you think?" I asked. "Should we give her brother a call?"

"Surely her mom called him first thing," he said.

"You'd think so. Although she didn't mention anything about it."

"True. Well, I suppose it couldn't hurt."

I called the number Aaron had given me, but it went straight to voicemail. I left a brief message explaining who I was, and hung up.

"It's definitely Mark Brown's number," I told Alex. "But he's not answering."

"You'd think with his sister missing he'd have his phone on," said Alex.

"Maybe he's in church."

"If I had a sister and she were missing, I'd leave my phone on, even in church."

"Yeah. Me too. Well, uh, what do you think we should do next? Should we go to the police?"

"We can if you want to. But she's been missing barely 24 hours. The police aren't going to be that interested yet. We can always go later. I say we wait. Especially since it sounds like Mrs. Brown recognized the car. Maybe it belonged to a friend or something. Let's give it at least a couple more hours to let her sort it out."

"Okay," I said. "Well, in that case..." My phone rang before I could finish my sentence. It was Matt.

"Professor Halley? We just got out of church. No one there knew anything. Like, they didn't even know of any other churches or anything that she might have gone to. Neither did Drew's friend who's a youth counselor. The only thing any of 'em could offer"—barely suppressed disgust dripped from his voice—"were their prayers. Shit. I'm probably going to Hell for saying that, and on the Sabbath, aren't I?"

"It'll be our secret," I said.

"Too late," he said. "Naomi's already smacked me for it. But look: church was a bust. You find anything out on your end?"

I filled him in on the car and the warehouse in Martinsville.

"Martinsville," said Matt when I was done. "That's, like, just a few miles down the road, right? Like, we could get there in half an hour, max, right?"

"Right," I said.

"Well, what are we waiting for? Let's head on over and check it out!"

"Um..." I said. "You think we should just barge in like that?"

"You got any better ideas?"

"What if no one's there? Or they don't want us there?"

"What if Ruth's there and needs help? What if she, like, I don't know, went there looking for help, and no one was there, and now she's alone and she needs someone to come get her?"

That seemed unlikely to me, but the possibility was so unpleasant I found myself half-agreeing with Matt that we had to go check it out.

"Let's meet at the bagel place," he said. "Ten minutes, okay? Then we can all head out together."

"Um," I said, but he'd already hung up.

31

"This is probably a bad idea," said Alex as we made our way back to the bagel shop.

"I know."

"It's a bad idea in and of itself, and it's an even worse idea to get those gung-ho meatheads Drew and Matt involved."

"I'm not disagreeing."

"But you're going to do it anyway, aren't you?"

"Maybe. What do *you* think I should do?"

Alex emitted a half-sigh, half-groan. "It's times like this I wish I still smoked, so I could stall for time by lighting up. And honestly? I kind of think we probably should go out there. I mean, what if Matt's right? What if Ruth went out to her family's place and, I don't know, blacked out and hit her head or something, and now she's lying there and she can't call for help and no one knows where she is. And what's the worst thing that will happen if we go out there? We waste an hour or two of our day driving out there, and potentially suffer some embarrassment when we show up and everyone's gathered there as one happy family and they give us side eye for breaking into their cozy group."

"Yeah," I said. "The potential for embarrassment is a major stumbling block for me. But I still feel like we should go check it out."

"Yeah. I just wish we could persuade Drew and Matt and Naomi to stay home."

But when we all showed up a few minutes later at the bagel shop, Matt, supported by Drew and Naomi, absolutely refused to stay behind.

"Either you tell us where she is, or we follow you there," said Matt. His face had gone an alarming shade of red as soon as I suggested that he stay behind and leave the trip to me and Alex. "No disrespect, Professor, but that's what I'm gonna do."

"Okay," I said. "Just play it cool once we get there, okay?"

"Sure, Professor. Whatever you want."

My faith in his ability to keep his word and play it cool if we actually got into something with Ruth's brother was low, but I accepted his promise as the best he could offer, and a few minutes later we were driving in a caravan of two towards Martinsville.

32

"I really wish I'd gone to the bathroom before we left," said Alex as we drove out of Bloomington. "All that coffee is really starting to make its presence felt."

"Ugh. Thanks for mentioning it." Now that Alex had brought it up, I was also getting low-level but persistent messages from my bladder, telling me I should have made a pit stop before setting off. Too late now. "There has to be somewhere we can stop on the way back," I said.

"If I make it that far," said Alex. "But somehow I get the feeling that if we tell Matt and Drew that we need to take a pee break, they'll just go charging in without us, and, I don't know, pick a big fight with Ruth's brother and mess things up even more than they're already messed up."

"Let's stop talking about it. Think about something else."

"Okay." Alex drove on in silence for a little while. We had left Bloomington behind and were now driving down an empty two-lane road that ran in a straight flat line between fields full of early June corn. A single red barn stood off in the distance, the only building within sight. It was a typical Midwestern scene, one that I had always found bucolic and comforting, but today the emptiness of the landscape, and the militantly straight rows of corn, held a queer air of menace. Or maybe it was just all the pee I was holding in backing up into my kidneys and giving me urea poisoning.

"So what do you think?" Alex asked, breaking the silence. "Do you think Aaron's right and Ruth ran off because she's pregnant? You think she and Matt did get it on, and now she's trying to figure out what to do?"

"If they did, she wouldn't know if she's pregnant or not yet," I said. "They only met last week. Besides, I snooped through his bathroom when we went to their place last night, and I found a box of condoms."

"Well, good for him. At least he's got some sense. Did you see how many had been used?"

"None. It was brand-new and unopened."

"So maybe he got them for show and then sweet-talked her into having unprotected sex. Or maybe she doesn't believe in using birth control and refused to use them."

"Or maybe he got them just in case, but it hasn't actually come to that. Maybe he doesn't want to rush into things and he's waiting for the right time."

Alex flicked a sideways glance at me. "Maybe," he said. "Although I think you might be projecting your own romanticism onto him."

"You might be surprised at how romantic men like him can be, under the right circumstances."

"Yeah. Doesn't mean they're good guys, even so."

"Yeah," I said. "Anyway, first of all, it's none of our business, and second of all, it's none of our business. I think this is our turn-off."

We followed the directions from Alex's phone telling us to turn right onto a one-lane road that ran perpendicular to the main road, taking us deeper into the corn fields.

"Is it just me, or does this look like a set for a horror movie?" Alex asked. "I mean, I know it's just corn, but it's creepy, right? Being surrounded by miles of corn higher than your head?"

"It's not actually that high yet," I said. "Although in a few weeks it will be. And yeah, now that you've said it, it's kind of creepy. But I'm sure we're perfectly safe. At least from corn."

"Yeah," said Alex. "Is that...yep, here we go. This is us."

The corn opened up to an old farmyard. There were several of the original wooden red barns scattered around the edges, and a modern warehouse-looking building with tan metal siding in the middle, where the main barn must have once been. Parked in front of it was a red four-door Yaris with Indiana plates that read 837 LIK.

33

Drew had been driving behind us the whole way, but now he cut around us and pulled up next to the red car in a spray of gravel. Matt jumped out of the car before Alex and I had even parked, Drew close behind him.

"Ruth!" Matt shouted. He went over and pounded on the warehouse door. "Ruth, you in there?"

Naomi, who had been sitting in the back of Drew's car, managed to disentangle herself from her seatbelt by this time and ran over to join Matt and Drew. I had to admire her commitment to her friend. I hoped no one was waiting on the other side of the warehouse door with a loaded gun. Not that I expected there to be a hardened gang of criminals lurking in there, but this was rural America. Everyone had guns.

"What if someone's got a gun in there?" I hissed to Alex, hoping to spread my fear around a little.

He made a face. "Good point. You stay in the car."

"I shouldn't sit back while everyone else runs into danger!"

"Yeah, you should. Because we need someone with enough brains to call 911 if something bad goes down."

"Good point. And jeez, see if you can get Matt to calm down a little, will you?"

Alex gave Matt, who was now threatening at the top of his lungs to kick down the door, a doubtful look. "I'll try."

Alex slid out of the car and walked over to where Matt, Drew, and Naomi were all shouting and pounding on the door. He said something quiet in Drew's ear. Drew slapped Matt on the shoulder, getting his attention. The four of them conferred for a moment, with Alex obviously laying out a plan that appealed to Drew and Matt but not to Naomi.

After a moment, the group broke up, with Drew, Matt, and Alex all setting off cautiously in different directions, Matt to circle the warehouse, and Drew and Alex to check out the outbuildings. Naomi came over and joined me with ill grace in the car.

"Gosh," she said, making the word sound much worse than it normally did. Of course, in her circle it *was* a very bad word. "I thought he—what's his name? Professor Miller—would be different than those two, but he sent me away too."

I shifted in my seat, hoping to find a position that minimized the pressure on my bladder. "Do you have any training in this kind of thing?" I asked.

"No. But how hard can it be?"

"In this situation, hopefully not very. But let's just sit here for the moment, ready to leap into action as Sisters of Mercy like the glorious women of the Red Army if necessary."

She gave me a sideways look. "And you're okay with this, Professor Halley? Somehow I thought you'd be insisting on being with them too."

"Maybe I have my own plan," I said.

Now Naomi was looking interested. "Oh yeah? What's that?"

All three men had disappeared, Drew and Alex into the outbuildings, Matt around the back of the warehouse. As if she had been watching and waiting, Ruth stepped out the warehouse door.

"To be ready for this," I said.

34

"**R**uth! Ruth! Come here! Come here quick!" Naomi had her head out the car door and was shouting at Ruth.

Ruth froze on the concrete pad outside the door, and turned to look back into the warehouse, like she was listening to someone in there.

"Come on, Ruth!" Naomi shouted. Then she bolted out of the car and took off towards Ruth.

"Aw jeez," I said. Naomi had reached Ruth and was holding her arm, talking to her intently. Ruth was half-listening to her, half-listening to whomever was in the warehouse.

Naomi starting dragging Ruth, who appeared unable to decide whether she wanted to stay or go, towards the car. A man stepped out from the warehouse and grabbed Ruth's other arm.

"Aw *fuck*," I said. The man was older and white, with short hair and nondescript features. I was guessing he was the man Sam and Brittany had both said they'd seen with Ruth. He talked to Ruth like he knew her and expected her to do what he said.

Now he and Naomi were getting into an argument while Ruth stood off to the side, looking miserable. At least no one was getting shot. Yet. But something about the man's expression was making the hair on the back of my neck stand on end. It was an expression I'd seen before, in people who were absolutely convinced of their own righteousness. He probably didn't go around mugging people and robbing banks. But he probably wouldn't hold back from violence if he considered it justified.

Ruth's here, I texted Alex. Then I got out of the car.

"You can't just disappear like that!" Naomi was saying to Ruth as I approached. "You can't just take her away like that and not tell anyone!" she shouted at the man. "Do you have any idea how worried we all were? How hard we've all been looking for her?"

"You were looking for me?" said Ruth. Her voice was barely audible, but she looked almost as pleased by the thought as she was surprised.

"Of *course* we were looking for you! We called the police and all the local hospitals! Even Professor Halley has been looking for you!"

"This ain't none of your business," the man said. "This is family business. It ain't nothing to do with you." He encompassed me in the glare he had been directing at Naomi. "Any of you."

"Not even Ruth's mother?" I said, coming over to stand next to Naomi.

"Ann's a good woman, but she's too softhearted to do what needs to be done sometimes."

"Like kidnap her own daughter?" I said.

"Ruth went of her own free will. Didn't you, Ruthie? Once we explained everything to her, she decided to do the right thing and come with us on her own."

Out of the corner of my eye, I saw Matt come around the side of the warehouse. Alex and Drew were approaching from the direction of the outbuildings.

The man saw them as well. "Stay back!" he shouted.

"Sorry, sir," said Matt, sidling closer along the wall. "But I'm here to make sure Ruth's okay."

"Is he the one?" the man asked Ruth.

She made a tiny shrug that might have meant "Yes."

"Mark!" shouted the man. "Mark, get out here!"

The door to the warehouse opened, and a man about Ruth's age stepped out. He was carrying a double-barreled shotgun.

35

"Whoa," said Alex. He and Drew were now within talking range of the rest of us. He held up his hands. After a moment, Drew did likewise. "There's no need for that," said Alex.

"I don't know about that," said the older man. "Seems like a man has a right to defend himself when strangers come looking for his daughter."

"They're not strangers."

"What?" The man, who was, just as I'd thought, Ruth's father, looked down at her.

"They're not strangers," she repeated, this time speaking a little louder than the whisper she'd used earlier. "They're my friends."

"You only just met them!" her father said.

"Yeah, but...they came for me. They thought I was in trouble, and they came looking for me. They must be my friends."

Her father was shaking his head in denial. "Your family's your friends, girl. Not these folks. They're not even in our church. You told me so yourself."

"Some of them are," said Ruth.

"Not the *real* church. Not the one you've been raised in."

"Close enough," said Ruth. "And the true church is in the heart, isn't that what you always taught me? The true faith is the one you carry around inside you."

Her father gave her an appraising look. "Maybe so," he said. "But you don't know these folks, Ruthie. You don't know what kinds of hearts they have."

"Maybe not," she said. "But how am I ever going to learn if I never go out into the world and meet people?"

"The world's full of bad folks, Ruthie."

"I know," she said. "But it's full of good folks, too."

"You don't know that these folks are some of the good ones!"

"But I don't know they're bad, either. And the only thing they've done so far is come looking for me when they thought I was in trouble. That makes them seem like good folks, doesn't it?"

"They just want to use you, Ruthie!" Mark jerked his shotgun in the direction of Matt for emphasis. "Stay back, man!"

Matt stopped his slow sidle in our direction, and held up his hands. "I don't mean any harm, man," he said. "I just want to make sure Ruth's okay."

"Why? So you can mess her up, defile her, all on your own?"

"Mark!" Bright red spots appeared on Ruth's cheeks. "How dare you? And that's none of your business anyway!"

"You're not denying it!" said Mark. "I'm right, aren't I?"

"You're wrong! I haven't...there's nothing..."

"Chill, man," said Matt, still with his hands in the air. "Nothing like that's happened." He looked to be blushing pretty hard too. One of the many bad things about purity culture was that, like Alex had said, it made you air your private business out in public.

"Yet," snapped Mark. "But it *will*, won't it?"

"That is not your business!" Ruth had actually raised her voice. "None of this is your business! And it's not Dad's business either! I'm a grown woman!"

"Obviously not, by the way you're acting," said Mark.

"Mark's right," said their father. "I know you think you're a grown woman, Ruthie, but you ain't acting like it. A grown woman wouldn't run off and cause trouble like you've been doing."

"You're right," said Ruth. "But the running off I've been doing has been with you. I ran off from *them*"—she nodded at Naomi and then at Matt—"I caused trouble for *them*. You just chose to poke your nose in my business and make me do things I'm ashamed of. You read those emails I sent to Mom about the fun I was having, the friends I was making, and you decided to come and drag me away. You never let me go out on dates when I was a teenager. You never even let me go on sleepovers when I was a kid. You never let me go *anywhere* or do *anything*. You didn't even want me to go to college, and you only agreed to it if I went to a Christian college in the same county where I'd lived my entire life. Well, I want to see more! I want to go visit different states—I want to go visit different *countries*! I want to go on that mission to Russia that I was telling you about—and I *will*! Because that's how you raised me, Dad: to go out and do good works and spread the Word and do what I think needs to be done. So I will. And if I want to make friends with people from a different branch of the church, or even a different church altogether, I will! And if I want to go out on dates, I'll do that too! It's time for me to put away childish things and become a woman, and that's what I'm going to do."

Ruth's father looked stunned, maybe by her declaration of independence, maybe by her excellent subversion of 1 Corinthians. "Ruthie..." he began.

"Don't let her fool you, Dad!" Mark punctuated his sentence with a menacing swing of his shotgun in the direction of Ruth and her father. "Don't let her trick you into overlooking this, this *sin*! You say you haven't sinned *yet*," he added, addressing Ruth directly. "But you *will*! I know how girls are! I know..."

"Just because Judith cheated on you, doesn't mean that all girls are like that," said Ruth. "And maybe if you'd been a little nicer to her instead of pushing her around all the time, she wouldn't have done it."

Naomi gasped. "Don't!" she cried, a split second before I saw Mark's finger tighten on the trigger.

"Don't!" the rest of us all shouted at once. "Put the gun down, Mark!" his father tried to say, but his words were drowned out by the sound of a shotgun blast.

36

Naomi threw herself on top of Ruth. I threw myself on top of Naomi. Someone, maybe Matt, threw himself on top of me. There was another blast, so loud it seemed like the air itself must have split open from the sound.

Joshua fit the battle of Jericho, and the walls came a-tumbling down flashed through my head.

"Ruth! Ruth!" Naomi was hissing insistently. "Are you okay?"

I opened my eyes. The only thing I could see was Naomi's pastel shirt. My face was pressed against her back and my arms were wrapped around her torso. Someone heavy was pinning us all down, keeping us from moving. My bladder was threatening to burst and leak all its contents down my legs if I didn't change positions immediately. There was the sound of swearing and fighting going on above us.

The gun's already gone off twice, I thought. *Mark will have to stop and reload before he can fire again.* That thought was less comforting than I hoped it would be. The unseen presence of the gun seemed to fill the air and all the sky above me, threatening to rain fire and death and divine justice down on us all, the guilty and the innocent alike.

"I'm okay," Ruth was whispering, sounding strangled. "I think. I just can't breathe."

I wriggled, clenching my bladder closed for all I was worth, until I got my face out from Naomi's back.

"Stay *down*!" Matt hissed in my ear.

"Ruth can't breathe!" I hissed back.

"Oh. Yeah." Matt slid slowly to the side, unpinning me and allowing Ruth to slither out from under the pile of bodies.

"Stay *down*!" Matt whisper-shouted at all of us again. "Don't move!"

Still lying flat on the ground, I risked a peek up at the struggle above us. Mark and his father were fighting over possession of the shotgun, with Alex and Drew trying to pull them apart.

It's not loaded, I told myself. *It's not loaded, it's not loaded, it's not loaded*. But I couldn't make myself believe it. It still felt as if the air itself were full of violent death, ready to tear us apart at any moment.

"Fuck, fuck, fuck," I could hear Matt whispering to himself next to me.

I inched over to him. "Can you jump up and catch Mark by surprise?" I whispered.

"And leave you and the girls unprotected?"

"I'll cover them," I said, more bravely than I felt. I was no stranger to being threatened by guns. But there was something about the random, scattershot nature of the shotgun that was freaking me out.

Matt gave it a second of thought, and then nodded decisively. "When I say 'Go,' try and drag them off to the side, and cover them, okay?" he whispered.

"Got it," I whispered back.

"Okay. On three. One, two, three—go!"

He burst up off the ground like he was on springs. I grabbed Naomi and Ruth and jerked them back. I couldn't get much leverage, lying down as I was, but they must have had the same idea, because all three of us went rolling wildly off to the side, out from under the fight that was going on above us. My bladder protested violently enough that I had to feel my pant legs to see if they were wet. No, thank God. Not yet.

As soon as she stopped rolling, Ruth jumped to her feet and took off towards where Matt was now tackling Mark. Naomi jumped up and ran after her. Well, I couldn't fault their courage. I got to my feet more circumspectly, concentrating hard on not wetting myself.

"Don't hurt him!" Ruth was shouting in the direction of where Matt and Drew were both grappling with Mark. I wasn't sure which "him" she was referring to. Maybe all of them.

Matt and Drew brought Mark down just as Alex pulled Ruth's father away from the fray. "Just take it easy," Alex was telling him, dragging him backwards. "Don't make it worse, okay?"

"Don't hurt him!" Ruth's father yelled as Drew and Matt piled on top of Mark, pinning him to the ground.

The shotgun went free in the scramble. Matt was trying to kick it away while holding down Mark's legs, and Mark was trying to grab it, and Drew was trying to pin Mark's arms in a bear hug, but Mark was fighting with the strength of someone who was crazy and didn't care whom he hurt, while Drew and Matt were obviously trying not to hurt him. Which was great, except Mark was in danger of getting free and getting his hands back on the gun.

Mark jerked his head back, smacking Drew hard in the face and making him loosen his grip. Mark got one arm free and lunged for the gun.

It's not loaded, I reminded myself. *But it's still a great weapon*, I thought.

Ruth must have had the same thought. She snatched the shotgun out of Mark's scrabbling fingers.

"Give me the gun, Ruthie!" her father shouted.

"No." She shook her head, and backed away from the fight. "Not till you all calm down."

Mark shrieked. Drew, whose patience must have run out after the headbutt, had twisted his arm into a painful-looking hold and appeared to be pressing firmly on a pressure point.

Ruth broke open the shotgun with practiced ease and looked inside. "Unloaded," she said. "Good. Dad, are you ready to show some sense?"

Her father flicked his gaze back and forth between her and Mark, who had now been flipped over by Drew and Matt and was being held facedown on the ground. "Yes," he said. He turned to talk over his shoulder at Alex. "You can let me go," he said. "I'm calm now. I won't do anything."

Alex looked over at Ruth. She nodded. He slowly released her father, who held his hands up.

"I'm sorry, Ruthie," he said. "I never meant it to get out of hand like this."

"I know," she said. "I know you did it out of love. And I've always trusted you, Dad. I've always trusted you to know what's best, and do the right thing. So now you need to trust me the same way. You need to trust *me* to remember everything you've taught me, and to act like you raised me to."

"Yeah," said her father. "Yeah. You're right, Ruthie." He held out his arms. "Can you come give me a hug?"

Ruth set down the shotgun and went over to him. They hugged each other tightly, crying a little.

Alex took advantage of the moment to slip around them and pick up the shotgun. He came over to me.

"You okay?" he asked.

"Other than desperately needing to pee, I'm fine. You?"

He gave the shotgun a look of deep loathing. "I fucking *hate* guns. Especially when people are pointing them at me. Eight years in the military only made it worse." He put one arm around me and kissed my temple. "Never a dull moment, though, am I right? Especially around you."

"I'm sorry you got dragged into this."

"I'm not saying we couldn't have been doing something more fun this afternoon, but I'd like to think we did something good here. At least I hope so."

I looked over to where Ruth and her father were still hugging. "Yeah, me too," I said.

37

After a while Ruth and her father separated and went over and convinced Drew and Matt to let Mark get up. They pulled him to his feet, but when he started threatening them, said they wouldn't let go of him just yet.

Then Ruth came over to where Alex and I were standing, while her father stayed with Mark. "Thanks," she said.

"No problem," I said.

She smiled a tiny smile. "That's what you say to everything, Professor Halley. Even when it obviously is a problem."

"Well spotted."

"Yeah, well, I guess I wanted to say thank you. For coming to get me. I know what I did wasn't very thoughtful."

Naomi came over to stand next to her. "You can say that again. Do you have any idea how worried we all were? How much running around we all did to try and find you?"

Ruth gave her a tiny smile too. "You keep telling me. I just never thought...I didn't think anyone would care, or even notice. Mark and my dad, they showed up just after you left, Naomi. I'd told my mom about, you know, how the four of us were going out and doing stuff, and she told them, and they...they got concerned for me. They were worried that I'd...stray, you know."

"They kidnapped you!" said Naomi.

"Not...it wasn't like that. They just came and said they wanted to talk to me, and we had to leave right now, they wanted to talk some sense in me, and they led me out of Ballantine and put me in the car and drove me here, and we've been here ever since."

"They kidnapped you," repeated Naomi.

"That's not how they thought about it. That's not how *I* thought about it. But they took my phone away, so I couldn't tell you what was going on."

"Kidnap," muttered Naomi under her breath.

"And it never even occurred to me that you would be looking for me," continued Ruth. "But you did. So thank you." She looked over at the shotgun in Alex's hand. "Do you mind if I put that away?" she asked.

"Please," he said. We all watched closely as she took the gun and, to our relief, carried it into the warehouse.

When she came back, gunless, Mark had calmed down enough that Drew and Matt agreed to let him go. Ruth went over and hugged him, and after a moment, he hugged her back.

"Well," she said, stepping back from him. "I think I'd better go." She looked over at me. "I've got class first thing tomorrow morning, and I haven't done any of my homework."

"In your case, I'll probably still accept it on Tuesday," I said.

"I want to get a start on it now anyway."

"Me too." Naomi laughed a little, letting out nervous tension. "And I'll bet Drew and Matt have a pile of homework too."

"Yeah," said Drew, rubbing his face, where a black eye was rapidly forming. "Come on, let's get you home."

Soon we were driving back through the corn, the four of them in Drew's car and Alex and I in Alex's car.

"Should we stop right here?" Alex asked, once we were back on the two-lane road towards Bloomington. "Avail ourselves of the corn? Or can you make it back to civilization?"

"We should pass a gas station soon. I can make it there. I think."

There was indeed a gas station a couple more miles down the road, and it was open and had a working bathroom. Sometimes it's the little things that matter most.

"You think it's going to be weird seeing them in class tomorrow?" Alex asked, after we'd gotten back on the road.

"Maybe a little. But we'll figure it out."

"Yeah." He reached over and squeezed my thigh. "You will. And maybe Ruth and her family will figure it out too."

"I hope so."

"And..."

I looked over at him. "Yes?"

"All this has been making me think. About us."

"How so?"

"It made me think that I really don't want to lose you, Rowena. Not just to getting shot or something, although fuck, that would be awful, so I'd take it as a favor if you'd avoid any more gun-wielding crazy people."

"I'll see what I can do," I said. "No promises, though."

"Yeah, I know. But there are lots of other things I could lose you to as well. Like working a shit job on the other side of the country. So I'd really like...I guess what I'm trying to say is that I'd really like for that not to happen. I'd like to make not losing you a priority."

"Thanks," I said. "Same here."

He glanced over at me. "Really?" His voice was surprised, but his face was smiling.

"Absolutely. I want to make not losing you a priority too. I want to make *us* a priority."

"Wow." He gave me another glance before looking back at the road. "That's, like, I don't know...it feels serious, doesn't it? Like we've got something serious."

"I know," I said. "But," I added, "not *too* serious, I hope. I'd hate for your creativity and enthusiasm—in *and* out of bed—to be stifled by our weighty declaration of intent."

"No worries there," said Alex. "As I have every intention of proving to you as soon as we get back."

"Is that a promise?" I asked.

He grinned. "You bet."

THE END

*Want to know what happens next? Get your copy of **Trigger Warning**, the next book in the series, by scanning the QR code below:*

*And as a special exclusive freebie for readers of **Summer Session**, you can get **Summer Break**, a short story set during the same time as **Summer Session** and told from Dima's point of view. You can also sign up for my newsletter at the same time (but only if you want to!) and get regular updates and offers. Get your free copy of **Summer Break** by scanning the QR code below:*

About the Author

S id Stark lives a life very similar to her characters', only with more grading and fewer exciting chase scenes. She did once get held up in Heathrow on suspicion of being a Russian criminal traveling on an American passport, though, which was fun. She loves to hear from her readers, and can be reached by email at **sidstark@sidstarkauthor.com**, at her website at **https://sidstarkauthor.com/**, on Facebook at **https://www.facebook.com/SidStarkAuthor/**, and Twitter at **@SidStarkAuthor**. You can also sign up for her newsletter by scanning the QR code below:

Don't miss out!

Visit the website below and you can sign up to receive emails whenever Sid Stark publishes a new book. There's no charge and no obligation.

https://books2read.com/r/B-A-NVEK-DMIFB

BOOKS 2 READ

Connecting independent readers to independent writers.

Also by Sid Stark

Doctor Rowena Halley
Campus Confidential: An Academic Thriller
Permanent Position: An Academic Thriller
Summer Session: An Academic Thriller
Trigger Warning: An Academic Thriller
Honor Court: An Academic Thriller
Total Immersion: An Academic Thriller
Under Review: An Academic Thriller

Doctor Rowena Halley Boxed Sets
The Doctor Rowena Halley Series Books 1-4: Four Dark Comedy
Mysteries